CW00435647

# Idwal's Bell

Lesley Pardoe

Illustrations by Lucy Rose Turner

# AD 994

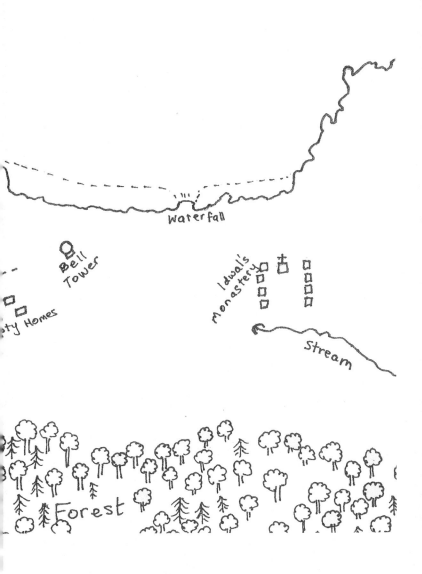

Waterfall

Bell
Tower

Idwal's
Monastery

...ty Homes

Stream

Forest

# Early Twenty-First Century

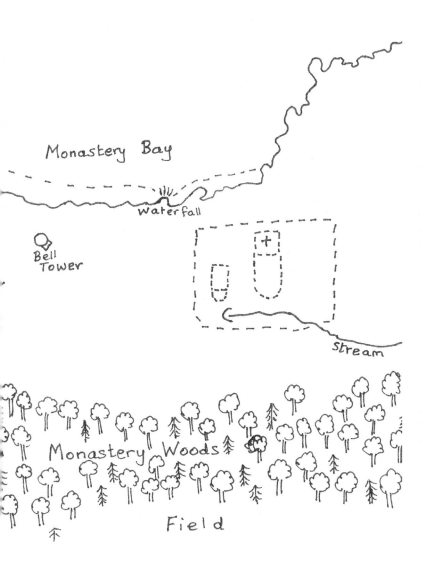

# Contents

For Milla

# Prologue
## AD 981

The little cluster of huts was ablaze. Fire thundered in the thatched roofs and the survivors struggling to drag out the wounded coughed and choked in the billowing smoke. Men and women, their clothing ripped and scorched and soaked with blood, lay dead and dying on the trampled earth, and next
to its mother's body a terrified child huddled sobbing.

A man hollered for his family, his hoarse voice straining against the roar and crackle of the flames, and a bewildered goat bleated as it trotted this way and that through the blackened wreckage.

1

# Idwal's Bell

Chest heaving, Gyffes stood at the seaward end of the village, his splintered ash staff in his scorched hands, watching as the raiders' ships, laden with wailing captives and plunder, pulled further and further out to sea. To his left the river rippled out undisturbed, but on the right, where the short grass gave way to sand, amid hundreds of scuffed footprints, trails and blotches of blood, lay the body of a man, a ripped cloak and a helmet.

Gyffes turned back to the burning huts where a few villagers laboured to douse the flames with water scooped in wooden buckets from the river. Steam plumed in vaporous curls to join the smoke. The heat tightened round him, stinging his eyes and suffocating his chest as he stumbled inland.

With a crackle and a roar, and a stifling shower of sparks, a hut collapsed beside him and he threw himself out of its way, grabbing a screaming child and shielding her with his body.

He looked down into the terrified eyes and croaked, 'Come on, Eywy, we'll find your Mahme. When did you last see her?'

The girl clutched his blood-stained tunic.

'I f-fell over. Mahme had th-the babies.'

# Prologue

'Then she'll come back.' And as they approached the far end of the roaring, burning settlement, a woman ran towards them, her long plait unravelling, and her skirt torn.

'Eywy! Oh, dear Holy Mother, my Eywy!'

The little girl let go of Gyffes and ran crying to meet her. 'Mahme! Mahme!'

Gyffes turned towards the hut he had come to find. The roof had collapsed, and flames licked greedily at the wooden frame. The caved in wattle and daub lay in smouldering heaps. Outside, Idwal, his hands bleeding and blackened, crouched over the body of his young wife. Gyffes's legs buckled under him and he reached out helplessly to his brother-in-law.

'Oh no,' he moaned, his parched throat choking him. 'Oh no, oh no.'

Idwal sobbed silently as he clutched the lifeless Morwenna in his arms, rocking her to and fro.

'No,' gasped Gyffes again, shaking his head. 'Oh no, no, no.'

'I was too late,' wept Idwal. 'My poor Morwenna.'

# Idwal's Bell

'And others,' growled Gyffes, his young face blood streaked and haggard. 'They were on us before we knew it. They've taken almost everything. Killed so many.' Idwal looked up, and Gyffes saw the jagged slash down one side of his face, oozing in a scarlet trail down his tunic.

'He got you!'

'And I smashed him with a stone. Too late, but I hurt him.' Idwal shook his head, tears streaming in pale rivulets through the soot and blood. 'He fell as they went. They had to carry him to the boats. But it was too late for her.' He bowed his head again, clasping Morwenna to his chest, the bright red from the sword cut dripping into her golden hair.

Gyffes grasped Idwal's shoulder and they sat in silence, Idwal still rocking the body of his murdered wife, anger, shock and grief pounding in their hearts. Then Idwal looked up, seeing Eywy clutching her mother, the survivors fighting to staunch the flames, and the pathetic, little goat as it turned and trotted and turned and trotted, trying to find its way in the crackling, smoking devastation.

Idwal's deep blue eyes looked straight into Gyffes's stricken ones as he vowed, 'We will never be caught like this again.'

# Chapter One
## Madame Rosa

'I dare you!' hissed Andy pushing his younger sister towards the fortune teller's tent.

'I don't want to,' protested Megan, wriggling away from him.

'You're sca-ared,' sung Andy, wrinkling his nose and waggling his head.

'I'm not! I want to buy another raffle ticket,'

'You can't. They're giving the prizes in a minute. Look! Everyone's going over for the prize giving.'

# Idwal's Bell

Mothers with babies in pushchairs, fathers, children and grandparents were all gathering close to where Mrs. Wishford, the head teacher, stood with a sheaf of papers in one hand and a microphone in the other. Megan pulled away from Andy's restraining hand and set off towards them, but Andy caught her wrist.

'Come on Megs! This is the only time there's been no queue! And if you wanted another raffle ticket, why didn't you buy two at once?'

*Why's it always me that's wrong?* Megan thought. Why *can't I get it right?*

'I asked for two,' she said, 'but the lady only gave me one and a pound back!' She searched in her pocket for the ticket. 'She wasn't listening.'

'You should've told her.'

'I did. She didn't hear me. She was talking to someone else.'

'Fate,' said Andy darkly. 'You're meant to go to Madame Rosa. Ask her if you're going to win the paint box.'

'I'll know in a few minutes,' said Megan, looking across to the growing crowd.

'You're sca-ared,' Andy taunted again.

'I'm not!'

'Go on then! Prove it!'

## Madame Rosa

Megan sighed. There had been a queue outside Madame Rosa's tent all afternoon, but now everyone had gathered onto the sports field for the prize giving. The school fete was almost over.

'Go on!' Andy urged, pulling her towards the tent.

Megan shook her head. The thought of the Fortune Teller made her flesh creep.

'I don't want to,' she said again.

'Wimp!' Andy's green eyes mocked her.

'No, I'm not!' snapped Megan, and sweeping the tent flap aside she stepped from summer sunshine into darkness as thick as smoke, while Andy chuckled outside.

She stood like a stone until her eyes had adjusted to the shadows. Over a scarlet silk veil, Madame Rosa's huge black eyes stared at her unblinking. Large ear hoops gleamed half hidden by her dusky curls and her crimson clawed fingers spread before her on the velvet- draped table. By her left hand was a deck of Tarot cards and by her right a crystal ball rested in its black cradle like a full moon in the night sky.

'Please sit down,' Madame Rosa said huskily. Megan fumbled with the velvet topped stool and then sat on it, her eyes fixed on Madame Rosa's, and put her pound coin on the table.

'Give me your hands.'

Megan offered them, palms upturned. Madame Rosa took them in her smooth, white hands and scrutinized the lines. Megan's heart fluttered.

'I see many pictures,'

'Will I win the artist's paint box?' Megan asked, her eyes brightening.

Madame Rosa glanced up at her and then stared at her palms again, moving her thumbs round the base of Megan's fingers.

'I see you like drawing and painting,' she said.

'Yes,' agreed Megan, thinking of all the sketches she did in school when she should have been concentrating on maths and science. 'Will I win the paint box?'

'There is a paint box,' said Madame Rosa, 'but not today.'

Megan sighed. Muffled slightly through the heavy canvas she could hear Mrs Wishford's voice announce, 'And the first prize goes to...'

'It could be years away,' she said, but

Madame Rosa pressed her palms and twisted her hands this way and that, peering at the lines on her fingers and feeling the base of her thumb.

'A long, healthy life,' she droned, 'with many friends and much travel. That's good.'

Megan thought, Anyone could say that, but Madame Rosa still stared intently at her hands, a frown wrinkling her brow.

'A journey towards water soon,' she muttered, while a smatter of applause followed Mrs Wishford's latest announcement.

'We're going to Eurodisney at the end of August,' said Megan, but Madame Rosa shook her head. She let go of Megan's hands and pulled the crystal ball towards her.

'I said 'towards water,' not 'across it,'' she said, 'and sooner than that.'

Megan frowned. 'We're not going anywhere till then,' she said, puzzled.

Madame Rosa blinked and turned the crystal ball slowly. She pressed her scarlet lips together and cupped the cradle in her long fingers, then shook her head.

'A journey towards water very soon,' she insisted, and then muttered, 'Someone there is very anxious, and there are shadows.'

'Shadows?' Megan leaned towards the crystal ball, fearful yet fascinated. It was clear and still.

'Ancient shadows,' whispered Madame Rosa, and turned the ball a little.

Megan's tummy turned over and she put her hands in her lap. Her palms were sticky and the back of her head prickled.

'Living water, living water,' mused Madame Rosa. 'The water is good.'

'Good? What do you mean?' Megan's heart beat fast, seeming to leap into her throat.

'The water is good,' repeated Madame Rosa. 'And there is something round and sharp and very old. Ancient.'

Megan's fists clenched. 'What is it?' she asked.

Madame Rosa shook her head and peered into the crystal ball, but she was listening too now, her head close to the shining curve. Fear washed over Megan like a chill rising tide.
Madame Rosa cried out, 'Someone running in terrible fear!'

Megan's eyes searched the shimmering ball. Was there movement in there?

'Who is it?' she asked.

'I can't see. I can only hear the footsteps.'

In the once clear crystal, Megan saw a writhing twist of cloud forming and reforming. She leaned closer and then gasped as through the moving mists a man's scarred face stared out at her.

## Madame Rosa

'Who's that?' she whispered, terrified.

'I can't see,' cried Madame Rosa, turning the crystal ball and searching it frantically. The deep blue eyes held Megan's as if calling her, telling her to come now. Megan's nails cut into her palms and she stared back.

'That man!' she cried. 'A man with a scar. There! Look!'

But the face was gone, and the ball was clear, gleaming in the darkness of the tent.

## Chapter Two
### Attic

'The woman's nuts,' said Andy as their mother drove them home. 'We're not going anywhere till the end of August.'

'I told her we're going to Euro Disney,' said Megan, rolling and unrolling her raffle ticket, 'but that's what she said.'

'She's just someone's granny,' continued Andy. 'You can read better rubbish in the stars in the newspaper,' and he leaned back and closed his eyes, stretching out his legs.

'You made me go,' pointed out Megan. 'You said it was fate. And she didn't look as old as that.'

'Okay, so she's someone's big sister. It's still rubbish,' insisted Andy, 'and I bet Rosa isn't her real name.'

'Actually, she's Miss Davison's cousin,' said
Mum, turning the car left into Hearn Avenue, and
then pulling into their drive. 'She does lots of fortune telling. But you're right. Her name isn't Rosa,
it's a strange name. Something like Ann or Anna,
but stranger than that. What's Dad doing?'

He was standing in the doorway of their
house, waving a phone at them.

'It's your sister!' he called.

'Oh! Perhaps she's had the babies,' said Mum,
pulling up the handbrake and hurrying into the
house.

'I thought they weren't due till August,'
said Megan.

'Unpredictable,' babies,' said Andy, sitting up.
''Specially twins.'

'Much you know about it!' retorted Megan.

'About as much as your fortune teller,' agreed

Andy, and climbed out the car, clutching the
coconut he'd won.

'Hi, Dad!'

'Hi Son,' replied his father. 'Good fete?
Great coconut!'

'Yep! What's all the fuss? Is it the twins?' He
stepped into the house, closely followed by Megan.

'No. Not yet. Uncle Rob's broken his leg.
They need help and Granny and Grandad can't go.
They're not back from America yet.'

## Idwal's Bell

'So?' said Andy.

'It's down to Mum,' said Dad. 'How about making a cup of tea?'

Andy groaned. 'I want to go on the X-box!'

'It won't hurt you to make a cup of tea first,' insisted his Dad. 'The X-box will still be there.'

'What are their names?' asked Megan, dropping her raffle ticket in the kitchen bin.

'We don't know. They're not born yet,' said Dad, selecting mugs from the cupboard.

Mum appeared in the kitchen doorway. 'I must go to them,' she said. 'Poor Rob fell from half-way up the ladder while he was fixing a drainpipe.'

'Go where?' asked Andy

'To help,' said Mum. 'They're in a dreadful spot. Rob's working while Liz is building up the bed and breakfast business. Rob'll have paternity leave when the babies are born, but now he can't put his foot to the ground. And they've spent all that money altering the house. They mustn't lose the summer's business. I think … yes, I think I'll have to take you two with me.'

'Why? We'll be all right here,' said Andy putting tea bags into the mugs, while Megan fetched milk from the fridge.

'Not while Daddy's at work,' said Mum, looking vacantly into space and thinking out loud.

14

Andy groaned again. 'Why not?'

Dad laughed. 'Because you'd spend the whole time on your X-box if there's no one here but Megan.'

'So?'

'You'll get fat,' put in Megan, 'You'll sit at the computer all day and stuff crisps and chocolate.'

'Shut up, Pain!' snapped Andy. 'Anyway, you'd just sit and paint and draw all day. What's the difference?'

'Painting and drawing don't dumb your brain like computers do,' said Megan.

'Only 'cos you haven't got one,' said Andy.

'That's enough!' warned Dad. 'When do you need to go, Love?'

'As soon as possible,' said Mum frowning. 'It'll be an awful rush, but do you think we could go Sunday?'

'Sunday?' echoed Megan. 'We'll miss the last three days of school!'

'I know,' said Mum, still thinking. 'I know you're not supposed to, but this is an emergency. And no, Andy, I am NOT leaving you here on your own. You and Megan can come and help. If there aren't any rooms free you can camp on the lawn. Anyway, you'll like it. Liz says it's a beautiful coast-line.'

'What?' said Megan, looking up. 'Coastline?'

'Yes,' said her mother turning to her. 'Liz and Rob live in St Idwal's. It's a seaside village.'
Megan gasped. 'Towards water!' she exclaimed.

'Oh, don't be silly,' said Andy. 'Britain's an island. There's water all round. Everywhere you go is towards water.'

But Megan's tummy turned over in fear, as she turned away. She hadn't told Andy about the scarred face in the crystal ball because she knew he wouldn't believe her, and now she wished she hadn't told him anything.

It was dusk by the time they reached St Idwal's on Sunday. Mum had insisted that Andy put away his Nintendo some time before so the children could see where they were going, but they saw little of the village as they wound through it, descending all the time. A church tower rose against a western sky still glowing long after sunset. Cottages lined the cupped hillside, shops clustered around the tiny harbour where a river ran out to sea and a pub sign swung under a streetlamp in the evening breeze.

'The Saving Bell,' read Andy, as the car passed. 'Funny name.'

Moments later Mum swung the car right and they travelled uphill again, away from the village on a broad track that led up on to the back of some cliffs. Darkness enveloped them and Megan yawned.

## Idwal's Bell

'We're almost there,' said her Mother. 'Aha! Look! Liz said it wasn't far from the village.' She pulled up before a white five barred gate.

They could just make out a low, two storeyed building with lights in several windows. A figure appeared in the doorway and hurried down the drive to open the gate for them. It was Auntie Liz.

'Hullo' she called as they drove through. 'Well done! You found us okay!' She pushed the gate shut.

'Brilliant directions,' said Mum. 'Get in!' I don't want you walking all the way back!'

Auntie Liz laughed but climbed into the back of the car next to Megan and directed them to a parking place.

'You've got lots of cars,' said Andy, counting four parked near them but Auntie Liz said three belonged to guests.

'What about us? Are we sleeping in the shed?' asked Mum.

'I thought about it,' said Auntie Liz, laughing again, 'but decided as you'd come to help, I'd better put you up somewhere proper. You've got a bedroom on the first floor Julie, and Megan and Andy have the attic.'

# Attic

'Attic?' echoed Andy, picturing rafters, dust and cobwebs.

'Yes. We're converting it into a guest suite, but we haven't decorated it yet, so it's a bit spartan.'

Minutes later they wheeled their cases into the entrance hall and Auntie Liz opened the door to the huge kitchen. A black cat lay curled up by a red Aga and down the centre of the room a long wooden table was laid with a red checked tablecloth, soup spoons and crusty bread rolls.

'Have you eaten?' asked Auntie Liz. 'I thought you'd like some soup before you go to bed. It's homemade tomato.'

Megan was about to protest that they only liked tinned soup, but it smelled so delicious she didn't say anything and ate it instead.

As she swallowed the last crumb of bread, Uncle Rob hopped through the door, leaning on a crutch.

'Hullo everyone,' he said. 'I thought I heard you come. Thanks for coming to help.'

He struggled to the table and sank onto one of the chairs.

'Rob!' exclaimed Auntie Liz. 'You only came home this afternoon, and you're supposed to have that leg up!'

'I can't lie down all day and all night as well,' grumbled Uncle Rob. 'I'm supposed to move around a bit. I've come to inspect the rescue party.' He turned and smiled at Andy and Megan, and Megan smiled back, hoping he wasn't always as grumpy as he sounded.

'So, you're going to help too? Well good,' Uncle Rob added as they nodded. 'There's plenty to do and I haven't finished that wretched drainpipe yet.'

'Well, if it can't wait, I'm sure Bethan's husband will do it for us,' soothed Auntie Liz. 'Bethan will be here in the morning to do the ironing,' she explained to Mum. 'She comes twice a week to help.'

'Of course it can't wait,' snapped Uncle Rob. 'That's why I was doing it. Now it's going to cost us money.'

'Can I do it?' offered Mum.

'No, Julie! Thank you but no.' said Auntie Liz. 'I'll ask Bethan if her husband can do it. Now, you two, what would you like to drink? You can have water in your bedrooms of course.'

Megan's eyelids drooped. 'I think I'd better go to bed,' she said, and her mother laughed.

'Come along then,' said Auntie Liz. 'I'll show you your attic.'

# Attic

They followed her as she waddled puffing up two flights of polished wooden stairs, pausing on the attic landing to show them the window.

'Fire escape,' she wheezed, pointing. 'And a view to the cliff top and you can just see Gull Island. Here are your rooms. It doesn't matter who has which. I'll leave you to settle in.'

'Wow!' said Andy. 'It's great!'

'Thank you, Auntie Liz,' said Megan. 'It's lovely!'

'Good!' said Auntie Liz. 'Now get some sleep and we'll talk more in the morning.'

'Good night,' called both children watching her go down the stairs.

Megan went to the landing window and looked out. She could make out a large, hedged garden below, and beyond the hedge the land sloped up to the cliffs, but there were dips and folds in the slope, and she couldn't see the cliff edge. Beyond the cliffs the sea glimmered and some way out a black hump rose from the water.

'Gull Island,' she muttered.

'Where?' asked Andy, coming to look.

'There,' said Megan pointing.

'Oh yes! It's quite small.'

'What's that over there?'

'Where?'

## Idwal's Bell

'There look. On the cliff. Some sort of building.'

'Probably another house. It's too dark to see.'

'It can't be a house,' puzzled Megan. 'It's like a tall thin tower.' She stared through the darkness, trying to identify the shape.

'Perhaps it's a lighthouse,' said Andy wandering off. 'We'll see in the morning. I'm going to bed now. Which room do you want?'

'It can't be a light house. It hasn't got a light. I can't make out what it is,' muttered Megan, feeling her spine chill.

# Chapter Three
## Building
### AD 981

Stone by stone the bell tower grew. Idwal's face was set in grim concentration as he laboured with the village craftsmen, placing the stones together and bonding them with mortar. On the beach below the cliffs, men, women and children gathered small rocks and large pebbles into cloth slings and leather buckets and trudged up the cliff path. Morgan had made a winch and a platform, supported by rope, which he lowered over the cliff edge to be stacked with stones by the workers below. The ropes and the winch creaked and groaned as he strained to turn the spiked wheel to raise the load, and the workers on the beach scurried out of its way.

## Idwal's Bell

On the cliff top, some distance from the edge, stood a tiny, new chapel, and to one side of it another group of men were building single cells to house the monks who would live in the monastery. Gyffes worked with them, thatching the wooden framed roofs with reeds cut from the banks of the river Ros that bordered the village.

'Somebody coming!' called Cadoc, who was mixing mortar on the landward side of the bell tower, and the builders turned to look.

Thundering up the steep path from the village came twelve horsemen. Their cloaks were tossed aside by the onshore breeze, and the scabbards and shields at their sides glinted in the sun. Already, Morgan was hurrying across the cliff top.

Idwal turned and shouted against the wind. 'Talek is here!'

Gyffes called the news to those on the beach below and they hastened to climb the cliff path. Everyone working on the new monastery hurried to the bell tower and stood in a whispering group. Talek raised a broad hand to halt his warband and surveyed the villagers as they gathered. Idwal and Gyffes walked towards him and bowed their heads as they drew close.

## Building

'Good day to you,' said Talek, looking down at them. 'You're working hard.' His gaze swept the cliff top, resting on the cells, the little church, and then measuring the half- built tower. 'A monastery?'

'We thought it best,' said Idwal. 'We have to build it quickly to seek God's protection from the invaders.'

'A monastery on the cliff top is easily seen,' said Talek.

The villagers glanced at one another and murmured.

'But the raiders already know we're here,' protested Idwal, turning to his companions. 'On the cliff the monks can keep watch. It'll be our vigil.'

'Your vigil? You're not a monk,' sneered Talek, his black eyes mocking as they rested on Idwal's face.

'I will be.  I hope I can earn God's help,' replied Idwal.

Talek looked at the woven silver brooch pinned to Idwal's tunic and touched the gold clasp that secured his own rich, blue cloak.  'Monks don't wear fine baubles,' he snarled.

'It was my wedding gift to my wife,' said Idwal.  'She was murdered by the raiders.'

'A fine gift. Where did you get it?'

'My brother is the smith in Tremarron,' said Idwal.  'He made it for me.  He melted together a smaller brooch and two rings that belonged to my grandmother.'

'And the stones?'

'One was in the first brooch.  The others I found on the shore, polished by the tide.'

Talek nodded. 'You're lucky it wasn't stolen. Was the man who scarred you the one who killed your wife?'

'Yes.'

'But he didn't steal her brooch?'

'He was taking it when I hit him.  I was too late to save her.' Idwal looked down.

There was a short silence.

'I believe I killed the man who killed my wife. I fear he'll be avenged.'

# Building

'By God, or by the raiders?' snapped Talek and his horse tossed its head and scraped a hoof on the ground as a hand tightened on the reins.

Idwal looked steadily back at him. 'Maybe they are the same.'

Talek's horse half reared and snorted.

'I've heard it said many times that the raiders are sent by God to punish evil doers in the villages they attack,' roared Talek. 'How have you made Him so angry?'

Many of the children huddled closer to their mothers. Their parents glanced at one another but shook their heads. There was a long silence before Idwal spoke again. 'We don't know of any evil doing in our village,' he said, his jaw tight. 'But we pray to understand why we were attacked, and so many of us were murdered and innocent children stolen from us.'

One woman gave a stifled sob and clung to her young son.

'I'm told fourteen of you died.'

'And five children taken for slaves,' growled Gyffes, glaring back at Talek.

'So those in the monastery will seek God's forgiveness and protection for themselves and the village? None too soon, I think! But I know some monks have moved inland when they've been attacked,' Talek jeered.

# Idwal's Bell

'It's too wooded inland,' retorted Gyffes. 'There are wolves, and maybe bears. The soil by the river here is rich, and we have water and the sea for fish.'

'Is the soil up here good for cultivation?' Talek raised his thick, black brows.

'Not as good as in the village, but good enough, and there is water.' Gyffes pointed across the cliff top towards the forest some way behind the new cells, where a rushing stream poured past them and plunged underground where the land sloped upwards to the cliff edge. They could hear it as it burst out from the cliff face and tumbled in a white cascade to the beach below.

Talek surveyed them from his tall horse. He glanced back to his followers, who sat, respectful, silent statues on their horses, poised for his next command, and then at the little stone buildings, the chapel and the tower.

'I'll send to Llandewi Monastery for some brothers to come to teach you. What else do you need?'

'More hands,' said Gyffes.

'And a bell,' said Idwal.

Talek looked at him again, at the scarred face and the bitter twist to the lips.

## Building

'Build your monastery then,' he ordered.
'And a strong defence for the village. If you run into
the forest when you are attacked, the wolves will
have the livestock. I'll send you more men. And a
bell. If the raiders return, you will save the village.
Do you hear me? You will save the village!'

He wheeled his horse around, and followed by
his warband, cantered back down the slope, while
Idwal, Gyffes and their companions watched in
silence.

## Chapter Four
### Blackcurrants

Megan woke with a jump to the frenzied ringing of a bell. At first she thought it was her alarm clock and groped for it before realising where she was and as she stumbled out of bed, the sound ceased. She sank down on the edge of the bed and rubbed her eyes, feeling her heart thudding with the shock, knowing her alarm clock sounded different.

Brilliant blue sky filled the square of the window and while she looked, a seagull skimmed across it. She stretched, thinking of her friends preparing for their last three days of school and crossed the landing to thump on Andy's door. To her surprise he was already dressed and listening to his ipod.

'What was that bell?' she asked.

'What bell?'

'Just now. It woke me up. I thought it was my alarm clock.'

'I didn't hear it. You must've been dreaming.'

'I wasn't. It made me jump.'

'Tinkerbell would make you jump.' He looked up. 'What sort of bell then?'

'Like a church bell. Only sort of, I don't know, frantic.'

'Nope,' said Andy, back with his ipod. 'Must've been just for you. Anyway, you said it was your alarm.'

'I only thought it was my alarm 'cos I was just waking up,' corrected Megan.

'Didn't hear a thing.' Andy stood up. 'C'mon. I'm hungry.'

Megan dressed and crossed the landing to stare out the window. There was the tall grey tower, partly hidden by the rise of the land, reaching up into the sunshine. It looked innocent and serene, but Megan shivered. It looks so old, she thought, and shivered again.

Twenty minutes later, as Megan and Andy ate their breakfasts, Mum outlined a plan.

## Idwal's Bell

'We've decided you two can do a couple of jobs in the morning and have your afternoons free,' she said. 'Okay?'

Andy groaned. 'All morning?' he asked, chewing toast.

'That depends on how quickly you work,' said Mum, frowning at him. 'Remember we've come here to help. And put that thing away. I don't want to see it while you're eating.'

Andy stuffed his ipod into his pocket and sighed.

'What do we do first?' asked Megan, cracking her boiled egg.

'Pick the blackcurrants please,' said Auntie Liz, waddling across the kitchen. 'Rob can strip them, and I'll freeze them.' She grasped the kitchen bench with one hand and stooped to open a cupboard. 'Here you are. Two plastic bowls.' She eased herself up and put the bowls on the bench.

'Don't pick each currant. Pick the stalk close to the stem so the currants stay in a bunch like grapes. That way you won't squash them. Thank you ever so much for doing it. I certainly couldn't just now!'

So, after breakfast, Andy and Megan went out into the big back garden and found the blackcurrant bushes in a large fruit cage. A strong post and rail fence backed by tall laurel hedges sheltered the garden from the wind.

# Blackcurrants

'C'mon,' said Megan. 'Let's get this done. I want to explore.' She looked up towards the cliff top, her tummy doing a strange little flip, but the hedge was too high for her to see beyond it.

They picked for an hour till their backs ached and the bowls were full, and Andy complained he had a dent in his thumbnail from digging into the stalks.

When they returned to the kitchen, Uncle Rob was sitting at the table, his plastered leg propped on a small pouffe.

'Okay guys,' he said. 'Hand over a clean bowl and a fork. This is my job.' He smiled at Megan and Andy. 'Never fall off a ladder,' he said, seeing Megan looking at his plaster.

'I'll try not to,' she said, liking his smiling eyes and brown hair, and glad that he was in a better mood this morning. She put her loaded bowl on the table, savouring the sharp scent of the dark berries.

'Smell good, don't they?' said Uncle Rob, sniffing. 'Yummy with raspberries in a crumble.'

He picked out a berry and squashed it, the dark juice trickling down his finger and thumb like blood, and Megan blinked and recoiled.

'I love crumble,' said Andy, ''specially the crumble bit.'

## Idwal's Bell

'Thank you, you two,' said Mum, coming into the kitchen with a laundry basket full of clean washing. 'I gather someone comes to do the ironing today.'

'Bethan,' said Uncle Rob, 'and here she is!'

A short round lady with greying brown hair appeared at the open back door.

'Hullo All,' she said, coming in. 'Sorry if I'm a trifle late, but my youngest had to go into Tremarron to the dentist suddenlike and I fetched young Gregory to come along o'me. You don't mind?'

'Of course not,' said Auntie Liz. 'Come in Gregory! Meet Megan and Andy.'

Gregory peered round the doorpost and stared at the redhaired green-eyed pair standing at the table.

'Wow!' he said. 'Celts!'

'What?' asked Megan.

'Greg!' exclaimed his grandmother.

'Well they are!' Gregory insisted. 'We've been doing Celts in school and they had red hair. You ask Miss Sutton.'

'Since you've broken up for the holiday, I can't,' said Bethan, 'but I think you could say "Hullo," nicely, instead of staring like that.'

## Blackcurrants

'Hullo nicely,' repeated Gregory obediently, and grinned, his brown eyes crinkling up at the corners behind large round spectacles.

'Broken up already?' said Megan. 'We don't break up till Wednesday.'

'Well your school doesn't,' said Mum. 'You're lucky because it's poor Uncle Rob who's broken. Not you!'

'It's an ill wind that blows no good,' quoted Uncle Rob. 'I'm happy to think by falling off a ladder I've given Megan and Andy a longer holiday. Go on you three. Go out into the sunshine. Get Greg to show you the old monastery and have swim in the cove. You could take a picnic, couldn't they Liz?'

'Good idea,' said Auntie Liz, coming in from the office. 'There are rucksacks in the stairs cupboard. Nectarines in the bowl, and some bread rolls in the bread bin. Fill them with what you like.'

'Monastery?' said Megan. 'Where's the monastery?'

'Up on the cliff,' said Uncle Rob. 'It's a ruin now, thanks to Henry VIII, but we hope it's going to be preserved and opened to the public to attract visitors to the village.'

'Is it to do with St Idwal?' asked Megan, feeling her hands go clammy.

'I believe so,' said Uncle Rob, stripping blackcurrants off their bunches into a colander ready for washing. 'I don't know much about him, but the story goes he was a monk who founded the monastery and by some brave and noble deed saved the village.'

'So he was a good man?' persisted Megan.

'Oh definitely a good guy. No need to worry if you see his ghost.'

'What? Really? Does he haunt the monastery?' Megan's heart seemed to be leaping into her throat. She swallowed.

But Uncle Rob laughed. 'No! Not that I've ever heard. Mind, we'd probably attract more visitors to the monastery if he did! No, you're more likely to meet Alan Wetherton. Go on! Go and enjoy the sun while you can!'

36

## Blackcurrants

'Almost bound to meet Alan Wetherton if they go up there around lunchtime,' put in Auntie Liz. 'I saw his Range Rover go up on Sunday, so he'll be there sometime this week.'

'C'mon Megs,' said Andy, tugging her arm. 'Come and get your swimming stuff.'

'Greg,' said Bethan, sorting washing. 'Have you got your phone?'

'Oh wow! Have you got a Smart phone?' asked Andy, turning round.

Greg pulled a small scratched object out of his jeans pocket. 'No,' he said, looking surprised. 'It's just a phone.'

'And it's the third one you've had,' said Bethan. 'He loses them like baby teeth.'

'That's exactly why we haven't given one to Andy,' said Mum.

'That's not fair,' said Andy. 'I wouldn't lose it.'

'Yes you would,' said Megan at once. 'You'd probably drop it down the loo.'

'You're not having one till September, when you change schools,' said Mum. 'Then you can tell us if you miss the bus home or something.'

'Yes,' said Bethan. 'Greg's got one so we know where he is.'

## Idwal's Bell

Greg stuffed the phone back in his pocket.

'C'mon,' he muttered. 'You get your things and I'll show you the bell tower and the monastery, and we can have a swim.'

Megan glanced at him. 'Bell tower?' she murmured, her heart still thudding.

'And a jumper or something,' called Auntie Liz as they hurried to the stairs. 'We do get these westerly winds off the sea.'

*That's what it was*, thought Megan. It was the wind making the monastery bell ring.

# Chapter Five
## Eywy's Nightmare
### AD 994

Gylan leaned his axe against the hut wall and began to stack the logs he had split. His father, Gyffes, had left him a pile of them to cut, with orders to do it properly. 'No daydreaming or chatting. I want it all done and stacked before dusk.'

Gylan wished he could measure up to his father's demands. He was always too slow, careless or forgetful. He grasped the axe and swung it. It bit into the wood, and he swung it again. The rhythm soothed his resentment, stretching his muscles and working his breathing to a steady in out flow.

Sometimes wood chips flew up and he gathered them for kindling. He picked up the logs and tossed them towards the hut.

His shoulders ached, and his hands were sore, but he was still working when his friends Conan and Branoc arrived and stood watching him.

'You coming up the river with us?' asked Conan, chewing on a hunk of bread.

Gylan shook his head. 'Got to finish this and stack 'em before dusk.'

''S nowhere near dusk yet,' said Branoc, squinting through his dark thatch towards the sun. 'You got plenty of time.'

'No,' said Gylan. 'I want to do it right. My tad'll be angry if I don't.'

Conan considered as he chewed. 'Won't take you long to get through that lot. You could easy do it after we come back.'

Gylan shook his head. 'We may be too late back. Tad'd be furious.'

'So what?' scoffed Conan. 'What's tanning? Are you scared?'

Gylan said nothing. He'd had a hiding many times and it hurt, but it wasn't that. He wanted Gyffes to be pleased.

'You're scared,' accused Conan, swinging his fishing rod round in an arc and whining, 'Going to get his backside tanned.'

'I'm not scared,' said Gylan, eyes down to what he was doing. 'I just want to get this right. I'm fed up with m'tad shouting at me.'

'Ooh, poor ickle Gylan,' mocked Branoc, grimacing.

'Shut up,' said Gylan, facing him. 'I've got to do this.'

'Bet it's not that,' sniggered Conan, digging Branoc in the ribs. 'He's waiting for his girlfriend.'

'I'm not!' protested Gylan. 'I'm working. I've got to finish the logs.'

''Course he is,' mocked Branoc. 'Should've thought. He's waiting for little Margiad.'

Gylan turned his back. 'Shut up,' he said again. 'Go and fish. I'm not coming.'

'C'mon,' said Branoc, tugging Conan's arm. 'Let's leave him to his sweetheart.'

'Yeah,' said Conan. 'She'll be along soon.'

Gylan ignored them and then turned to watch them as they walked off giggling. He loved fishing and Mahme would have been pleased with the fish for supper. Resentfully he swung his axe for another half hour and bent to pick up the logs.

'Gylan!' A voice whispered behind him.

# Idwal's Bell

He spun round and there was Margiad, as sudden and as quiet as a windblown leaf, her red hair tumbling tangled over her shoulders and her slight form crouched to avoid being seen.

'You made me jump!  Why did you creep up like that?'

'I want to show you something.'

'What?  Why are you whispering?'

''Cos I don't want anyone to hear.  Have you finished the logs?' She looked at the untidy heap.

'I've just got to stack them.  What is it?'

'Can't tell you now.  We've got to find it.  I'll help you stack.'  She picked up a log in each hand, gripping her small fingers round the girth of wood.

'You have to do it properly, so they don't slip,' said Gylan, pushing her aside.

'I know!  I'm not stupid!'

'Just pass them to me.  I'll stack them.  Why are we in such a hurry?'

'It's a long way and we don't want anyone to know,' said Margiad, gathering logs. 'If we're not back before supper, they'll know we've been out.'

'Out where?' asked Gylan, straightening up and wiping his long flaxen hair out of his face.

'Just bring your staff.'

Gylan settled the last log in place and straight-ened up.  'The forest?'

'We're not supposed to go there.'

'Sh!' Margiad glanced round. There was no one about.

'That's why I said bring your staff. You'll want to see what we're going to find.'

'Don't you know where it is?'

'Not exactly. Come on! There was no one on the fortifications near the bridge when I came. I checked. And Yestin's not out with the cows.'

Gylan looked at her for a few moments, his blue eyes serious, trying to work out her mood. Theyhad been companions since they were small, and she joined in all his exploits, fishing in the river and at the sea's edge, climbing the cliffs near the monastery in search of pungent rock samphire, or gathering winkles in Monastery Bay. She had never urged him to go up into the forest above the river before. She was as afraid of wolves as he was.

She crept to the front of the hut and looked up and down the path. Then she beckoned.

'Come on!' she hissed. 'There's no one in sight.'

Gylan grabbed his staff from where it leant against the hut and strode ahead of her.

'Come on then,' he muttered. 'We'd better be quick.'

# Idwal's Bell

They dashed across the path and wove their way between huts towards the tall fortifications, built years ago. The gates were not barred, and they opened, creaking, and creaked again as Gylan pushed them shut. They scuttled across the wooden bridge where the river Ros battled with the high tide and flung themselves down near the six cows who chewed placidly in the spring grass. They looked back towards the village but could see no one. Without a word they scrambled to their feet and ran up the slope towards the edge of the forest that cloaked the steep hillside. Gylan glanced behind to see if they had been spotted, but Margiad kept running till she reached the first trees.

'I don't know exactly where it is, but I think it's round here a bit,' she puffed, making her way to the left along the edge of the woodland. Then where an oak dropped low to meet the slope she turned into the trees, trotting and jumping over the undergrowth like a young deer. Gylan followed, keeping sharp lookout as the shadows deepened.

'Don't make too much noise,' he warned. 'I don't even know what to look for.'

'We'll both know when we see it,' said Margiad, picking her way along a faint trail, that showed traces of being covered up with a bent branch here and scattered leaves there.

They jogged steadily upwards, breathing more and more heavily, till Margiad stopped and Gylan bumped into her and looked over her shoulder.

Halfway up the steep, forested hillside was a large clearing, bounded by a high wooden fence. Gylan stared at it, astonished.

'See?' said Margiad. 'I knew it was here.'

'How did you know?' asked Gylan. 'No one's told me.'

'No one told me either,' said Margiad, putting a small white hand on one of the wooden rails. 'Eywy had another nightmare last night and woke up. I heard Mahme telling her about it.'

Gylan put both hands on one of the rails, and a foot on the lower one. 'Easy to climb,' he said, 'but there must be a way in.'

Margiad walked a little way around the fence. 'It's here,' she said. 'Look. This bit comes out to let the animals in, and then we shut it after them.'

'There could be wolves,' said Gylan, looking around. 'We shouldn't be here.'

'I know,' said Margiad, 'but we're together. And if we have to bring the animals here there'll be lots of us to scare the wolves.'

## Idwal's Bell

Her green eyes looked darker in the woodland, and the leaves made moving patterns on her pale face. Gylan turned away, dropped his ash staff and climbed the fence. It was almost twice his height, and the rails were close together.

'A wolf couldn't get into that,' said Margiad.

'But if it's full of animals, there won't be room for us,' Gylan pointed out. 'Everyone would have to carry sticks with them.'

'Only the women and children come here,' said Margiad. 'I heard Mahme say the men stay and fight.'

Gylan turned and looked down at her, his straight blond hair swinging forwards. 'Then I'll stay and fight!'

'You're not a man!' said Margiad. 'Twelve isn't a man!'

'It is nearly!'

'You wouldn't know what to do. We're not even supposed to know about it.'

Gylan began a slow descent, thinking as he came.'I hate not knowing,' he said. 'It's worse than knowing. Nobody tells us anything. What did you hear?'

He slithered down the last few bars and sat on the fragrant forest floor and Margiad sat next to him breathing in the mingling scents of leaf mould and violets.

'Not much,' she said. 'I told you; I heard Eywy crying in the night.'

'Nightmare.'

'Yes. I'm not supposed to know what it's about, but I do. She dreams she's being dragged away by the raiders, and everything is burning.'

'It was before we were born.' He scrunched a dead leaf in his fingers.

'She still has nightmares. Mahme was telling her about this place. She was saying we can run here with the animals and hide, and they won't find us.'

'So they really think they'll come again?'

Margiad shrugged. 'Morgan doesn't. I asked him. Nor Cadoc. Mahme won't say.'

'Nor will mine,' said Gylan. 'She just says I mustn't think about it. But look at the fortifications. They've even been making the bottom bit stronger with stones. They should tell us what to do if it happens again.'

'Cadoc was grumbling about building the stone bit,' said Margiad. 'He says it's a waste of time now Talek won't send us any more helpers. He thinks nothing will happen.'

Gylan plucked a violet and rolled it between his finger and thumb.

'But Talek did send them at first. They helped to build the monastery, and he used to come often to make sure we weren't making God angry. He was worried about it then all right.'

'I don't see how we make God angry,' Margiad said, twisting violets into a circlet. 'I think it's the raiders who're bad. Not us.'

Gylan gasped. 'You mustn't say that,' he said. 'You'll make Him angry just saying that! And He'll punish us.'

Margiad slipped the purple petalled bracelet onto her wrist and looked back at him. 'If God really sends the raiders nothing can stop them. Yet we've built a monastery, and the monks keep watch up by the waterfall, and we've built the fence round the village, and now this.' She nodded towards the cattle pen. 'What's the use, if God's angry with us? But the raiders are thieves and murderers. No one in Porthros does those things. Why doesn't he punish the raiders?'

'Maybe He has punished them, but we don't know.'

'If He has, they wouldn't dare come back. Why've we done all this?'

'Idwal's made us,' said Gylan. 'He's a monk and he should know.'

Margiad smiled. 'Idwal and your tad. But your tad still doesn't tell you anything.'

Gylan stood up. 'He doesn't want me to be scared,' he said. 'Come on. We shouldn't be here,' and with Margiad following, he hurried back along the narrow path.

They jumped over fallen branches and swished through last year's rotting leaves now punctuated by flowers springing up from beneath the decaying litter. They wriggled through a hawthorn thicket and Gylan stopped and Margiad cannoned into him.

'What is it?' she asked.

'I thought I heard something.'

'What?'

Gylan held up his hand and whispered, 'I'm not sure. A swishing sound. Like something pushing through leaves.'

'Us?' breathed Margiad, but Gylan shook his head.

They waited. Margiad shifted her feet to a more comfortable position and Gylan waved his hand to make her keep still.

'I can't hear anything,' she muttered.

'Shush!'

There was a long silence, and Gylan crept forward. A twig crackled. He stopped. Margiad grasped his tunic. For slow minutes they stood motionless, holding their breath.

A breeze rippled the new leaves and the sunlight flickered. Gylan groped for his staff, realising with a surge of panic he'd left it by the enclosure. He looked round for a strong stick, but the undergrowth was dense.

'You irresponsible fool,' his father's voice echoed in his head. 'Think ahead. Think for yourself. Stop behaving like a child,' and Gylan knew his carelessness endangered them both.

'It was the wind,' hissed Margiad, as the leaves stirred, but Gylan shook his head again. Silence settled round them like a shroud. Gylan could feel Margiad's breath on his neck and his own heart beating. He took another step forward and spread his hands on an old oak tree. Had the sound been Margiad after all, or someone else? He listened, tensing as she stepped up close behind him still clutching his tunic. He edged round the tree and froze.

Directly ahead, with yellow eyes glowering, stood a large grey wolf.

'Holy Mother!' gasped Margiad.

## Idwal's Bell

There was calculation in the wolf's staring eyes. It snarled. Its hackles rose and it lifted its tail.

Gylan fought to hide his fear, but his blood roared through his body, thundering in his ears and shaking his limbs. He put out a hand behind to keep Margiad back and his eyes searched the undergrowth for a stick. The branches lying on the ground were all rotten. The wolf's lips curled back from its yellow teeth and Gylan could see that some were missing. He noted the visible spine and ribs, the concave dip before the lean hind quarters, now taut, ready to spring. This wolf was old; was detached from the pack. It was hungry. Desperate.

Gylan's heart mounted into his throat. Margiad made no sound behind him, and he knew she was rigid with fear. He had only seconds, and Gyffes's voice still echoed in his head. 'Look into its eyes. Never turn round.' Gylan swallowed, searching his peripheral vision. A broken off branch lay close to the wolf under an overhanging spray of hazel. Supple hazel, though it was at least a year old.

'Oh God, help me now. Help me get it right,' he prayed silently.

He curled his toes in his leather boots and stretched them again, crunched up his calf muscles, bent his knees and sprang for the hazel branch, wrenching it back and letting it go so that it whipped forward and struck the wolf who recoiled. Gylan reached forward and grasped the broken branch, re-alising too late it was hawthorn as the prickles sunk into his palms. He yelled, 'Get back! Get back!' and leapt at the wolf, waving the branch at it and catching it on the snout. The wolf snarled and arched its back, but Gylan struck it again and it turned and ran down the narrow path, glancing back once and then loping resentfully through the undergrowth.

Gylan grabbed Margiad's hand and followed it, dragging her behind him. A little way further on and she pulled him sideways.

'Here, down here. It'll be quicker,' and he marvelled at her quick thinking.

They crashed left, both stumbling into broken twigs, rotting leaves and wild garlic, squeezing through hazel branches and brambles and skidding down a steep slope, their feet shooting out from under them so that they half slid, half rolled through the tangled woodland to a steep mossy bank where water seeped from the ground.

## Idwal's Bell

'Get up! Get up!' yelled Gylan, pulling Margiad to her feet and they crashed and racketed downwards until they came to the edge of the woodland and the grassy meadow where the cows grazed.

They crouched in the undergrowth, peering through branches not yet in full leaf and surveyed the little settlement in the valley below. The river Ros still fought against the high tide, and beyond it, protected by a circle of fortifications was the cluster of huts, most of them rebuilt with stone since the Viking raid, but some of wattle and daub which would not burn easily. There were no wooden ones now, but all were thatched. Smoke rose lazily from some of the roofs. Yestin was calling the line of cows over the bridge into the village after the day's grazing.

Gylan and Margiad flattened themselves panting in the grass until the cows had gone and then sat up. They turned round, fearful of seeing the wolf pack behind them.

'There's bound to be a pack. They must have heard us,' said Margiad, shivering, as she brushed leaves and clinging twigs and brambles from Gylan's tunic. 'Get these off or everyone'll know straightaway where we've been,' she said. 'You were so brave.'

'I didn't know what else to do,' muttered Gylan. 'I left my staff up by the enclosure. I ought to go back for it.'

'No,' said Margiad horrified. 'They'll come after you! I've never been so close to one before.'

'Nor me,' said Gylan, shivering again. 'I thought we'd had it. Don't tell Tad. He'd be furious.'

''Course not. And you can soon make a new staff. He won't know.'

'He will. I made a pattern on it. I won't be able to get it the same.'

'Will he notice that?'

'Yes,' sighed Gylan. 'He notices everything.'

Margiad was silent. Gylan saw in a detached manner that his hands were still shaking, and that trickles of blood ran from the hawthorn wounds.

'I was scared,' said Margiad. 'I thought we were going to be killed.'

'Me too,' agreed Gylan. 'And we couldn't run away. The undergrowth was too thick.'

'And then the pack may have come, hearing all the noise. You were so clever to think of doing that.

'We were lucky the branch was there,' said Gylan, rubbing his hands together to stop them shaking and smudging the blood.

Margiad shivered. 'If you hadn't grabbed it first go...'

'Don't,' said Gylan.

Margiad wrapped her arms round herself.

'Well, we found what we went looking for,' she said. 'People do think the raiders will come again.'

'The Sea Wolves,' said Gylan. 'I heard Mahme call them the Sea Wolves once. So there are wolves that attack from the sea to kill us and steal, and wolves that live in the woods. We're surrounded.'

'I think we should go home,' said Margiad.

They wriggled down the hill to the cows' pasture, and still ducking low they ran to the river. As they crossed the water and went through the fortifications, Margiad puffed, 'We should go and ask Anhellis. She always knows everything.'

'All right,' agreed Gylan, bending over to regain his breath. 'How does she know everything though?'

'I don't know,' said Margiad. 'Eywy says she's got special powers, but Mahme says she's just gifted. Come on. You don't want to be late back.'

Anhellis's hut was on the edge of the village and they could smell the smoke from her cooking fire outside her door. Margiad knew she put dried herbs on it. Now she was brewing a soup made from chicken bone stock and wild garlic leaves. Gylan savoured the aroma. 'Smells good,' he said, as they approached.

Anhellis looked up from stirring the brew and smiled, her teeth gleaming in her wrinkled face.

'First garlic I've picked this year.'

'Mahme won't let me pick it till it blooms,'

'Ah. Because the leaves look like other poisonous leaves.'

'Yes. But I think I do know the difference now.'

'Better safe than sorry,' said Anhellis, tapping her wooden spoon on the edge of the pot and then putting it down on a stone, 'though they do smell different too. Now what can I do for you two?'

'We don't only come to see you when we want something,' said Margiad, and Anhellis laughed, shaking back her long, grey plaits. 'No, you don't she agreed, 'but it was the way you came. No smiles, slowly as though you were creeping up on the truth.'

'You didn't see us coming till I said your soup smells good,' said Gylan.

'I saw you in my mind's eye.'

Gylan and Margiad glanced at one another.

'Can you see a lot in your mind's eye?' Gylan asked.

Anhellis chuckled like a nattering gull.

'Not as much as people think. Depends who wants to know. Why would you two want to know what's in my mind's eye?'

# Idwal's Bell

Gylan sighed. 'Because we don't know what's going to happen,' he said.

'None of us does.' Anhellis picked up her spoon and stirred slowly. Steam rose from the soup. 'We're not meant to know.'

'But you do sometimes,' said Margiad. 'You always know when there's a storm coming.'

'Because I've learnt the signs. Anyone can do that. They learn to feel it in their bones.'

'And you knew when Ayla was pregnant.'

'That didn't take much working out,' retorted Anhellis. 'There she was with bright eyes and saying she could smell everything too strong. That was easy.'

Gylan was digging holes in the soft earth with a stick. 'But sometimes you know other things,' he said, not looking up.

Anhellis glanced at him and then looked down at her soup again.

'I know what you want to know,' she said. 'And I know that because you two have always want-ed to know everything. Not like some idle folk I could mention.' She glowered into the soup. 'There are those that don't care, or hide away from hap-penings past, present and future. I always wanted to know. And always will.'

She pointed her spoon at Gylan and Margiad, her faded eyes holding theirs, and for an instant Margiad could see her as a young woman, with raven black curls swept away from great dark eyes.

'You learn what might happen, and mind, I say, 'might' happen,' Anhellis smiled again, 'by watching others – how they behave, and react to what happens to them. When you see that, you can guess what they might do another time. Your father,' she nodded to Gylan, 'teaches you well. However hard he is, you mind him. He cares.'

Gylan lowered his eyes and watched the fire flames licking at the blackened pot.

'What about Idwal?' he asked, looking at Anhellis again.

'Brave man,' said Anhellis, nodding. 'Brave, stubborn man. I saw him coming down to talk to your tad a little while ago.'

'Did you?' asked Gylan, looking up. 'Oh good! I must go and see him! Come on Margiad.'

'I just hope your tad listens to what he has to say,' Anhellis said.

'He does,' said Gylan. 'They argue, but they usually sort it out.'

'I pray to God they do,' muttered Anhellis, stirring again.

'We'll come and tell you,' promised Margiad, and Anhellis laughed.

'I shall know before you get here,' she said. 'News travels faster than you can. And they don't tell you anyway.'

As they walked to Gylan's home, Margiad said, 'She knew we were coming before we came.'

'I've been thinking about that,' said Gylan. 'I think she saw us go up to the forest.'

# Chapter Six
## Picnic

Megan, Andy and Greg puffed up the grassy track to the top of the cliff. Ahead of them and to their right lay the tumbledown walls and arches of the ruined monastery, with its separate bell tower much closer, rising dramatically into the blue sky. To their left were the cliffs and the wide expanse of the sea.

'Wow!' breathed Andy, while Megan rummaged in her rucksack for sketchpad and pencil.

'What's that noise?' she asked.

'That's the waterfall,' said Greg. 'It's over there, where that man is.' He pointed to the cliffs beyond ruins. 'Come on! I'll show you.'

'Ought we to?' Asked Andy, catching up with him. 'We don't know that guy.'

# Idwal's Bell

'I do,' said Greg. 'It's Tom Merthen and my Mum works for him in the tourist office. He's a great guy.'

He headed towards the man who was sitting cross legged above the waterfall, a short distance back from the cliff edge, and after a moment's hesitation, Megan and Andy ran after him. They could see Tom Merthen greeting Greg, who sat down next to him, and as they approached, he turned towards them.

'Hi,' he said, smiling. 'I gather you're part of the rescue party for Rob and Liz.'

'Yes,' said Andy, shaking the outstretched hand, and raising his voice against the sound of the falling water, while Megan stared at Tom's dark blue eyes. She had seen eyes like that before, surely... 'Well Mum is. We're just helping. We've only picked fruit and veg so far.'

'Well, harvesting's important,' said Tom. 'The world would starve without it, eh Greg?' Greg grinned up at him. 'Greg's dad is a fisherman, so he knows all about that.'

'Oh,' said Megan. 'We didn't know, but I s'pose there's lots of fishermen in St Idwal's.'

'Not nearly so many as there used to be,' said Greg. 'My Dad says when he was a boy, fishing was huge. It's not now. That's why we've got the tourist office isn't it, Tom?'

'Yes. We need all the visitors we can get, or there won't be any jobs here and the village will die. We already have lots of houses owned by people who only come occasionally for weekends and holidays.'

'Is that bad?' asked Megan.

'Well, it means there are fewer local people here. So there are fewer children in the school. Fewer people buying from the shops. Less work for others to do. Difficult to keep a village going like that.'

'That's sad,' said Megan.

'We're fighting it,' said Tom, smiling. 'It's a good place to be.'

Megan and Andy walked a few tentative steps towards the cliff edge. They weren't sure how steep the cliffs were. The waterfall showed them. About a metre and a half from the top of the cliff it roared out and cascaded to the beach below, darkening the rocks around it. A rainbow hovered at its foot where the spray leapt up from tumbled boulders before rippling across the sand to the sea.

'Wow!' breathed Andy again, gazing at it in awe. 'That's amazing!'

Megan lay on her tummy and wriggled forwards, peering over the edge.

# Idwal's Bell

'Come back! You are too close,' said Tom. Megan wriggled back and turned towards him.

'I like to watch the water gushing down,' she said, staring into the intense blue eyes, and the words echoed in her brain as though she'd heard them before.

Tom smiled. 'But best not go down with it,' he said, and Megan slid further back.

'Where does it come from?' asked Andy.

'From the hills over there,' said Tom, pointing to a belt of trees behind the monastery. 'It goes under ground in what used to be the monastery garden. It was walled at one time, and I want to restore it. The monks would have used the stream for their fresh water.'

'Funny place to build a monastery,' said Andy. 'It's windy now. It must have been freezing in the winter.'

Tom laughed. 'Probably,' he said, 'but Idwal founded this monastery to protect the village, so it had to be somewhere he could look out to sea.'

'What do you mean?' asked Andy.

'I know,' said Greg. 'The village was attacked by the Danes!'

'That's right,' said Tom. 'They built the monastery up here, so the monks could see if the Vikings were coming. Then they could ring the bell and warn the village.'

Megan looked across the grass towards the bell tower. She imagined the Vikings sailing over the horizon and Idwal running to ring the bell across the same short, grassed turf before them now. The hairs on the back of her neck rose and her hands clenched.

'I suppose,' she murmured, 'we're sitting in exactly the same spot as Idwal sat, waiting for the Vikings?'

'Yes indeed. Though I imagine there was as rota system to keep watch.'

'How long ago?' asked Andy.

'Over a thousand years now.'

'Wow!'

For a few moments they were all quiet, gazing out to the rocky hump of Gull Island and watching the seagulls wheeling and gliding over the cliffs, calling to one another.

'How do we know?' asked Megan.

Tom smiled again.

# Picnic

'The story was well documented at one time,' he said. 'We have a few fragments of an ancient manuscript. It has a beautiful woven celtic design on it and mentions someone called Gylan. We don't know who he was – possibly a messenger. But of course, Henry VIII's men caused most of this damage to this monastery. It wouldn't have been in this style in Idwal's time. The ruins here now are what remains of a much later building. But it was still the same monastery. Unfortunately, Henry VIII's men also destroyed nearly all the manuscript.' He sighed. 'But we'll use whatever we can to preserve it for future generations – if we're allowed to. It's a pity Idwal isn't here now. If he still wants to preserve the village and monastery, something's got to happen soon.'

Megan looked at him, feeling the blood drain from her face and her body grow cold. For a few heart stopping moments she could see Idwal sitting right next to them, crosslegged, staring out across the glittering water.

Tom glanced at his watch. 'And now I must go.' He stood up. 'I wanted to see Alan Wetherton, but he's later than I thought he would be, and I have to get back to the tourist office. Nice to meet you!'

He smiled and nodded at them all, his brown curls whipping about in the strong breeze. 'Have a good swim!' He turned and strode back towards Auntie Liz's house, down the path that led to the village.

'Who's Alan Wetherton?' Andy asked Greg.

'Oh, he's a weird guy who brings pony trekkers up here for lunch,' said Greg. 'He runs a trekking centre, and the monastery is about halfway through his trek.'

'What's weird about that?' asked Andy.

Greg shrugged. 'I just don't like him. He's grumpy. He brings drinks up here and stores them in the old monastery kitchen, so the riders don't have to carry them. That's why he doesn't want the monastery to be preserved and turned into a museum. Mum told me he wants to buy it so nobody else can use it. He's a right poser. He's got a posh motorboat and a tender that he uses to go fishing round the island. Anyway, do you want to swim? You can see the waterfall better from the beach.'

He led the way at a canter down a path some way to the left of the waterfall, edged with wiry grass, sea pinks and a few small tamarisk bushes, and they scattered across the empty beach, turning to look at the waterfall when they reached the sea's edge.

# Picnic

'When there's a high spring tide it falls straight into the sea,' Greg told Megan and Andy.

Neither of them knew what a spring tide was, but they were impressed by the sight.

'It's not that it's particularly big,' said Andy, musing, 'but it's such a surprise to see it there.'

'Shucks! Now I've got wet feet!' yelped Greg, hopping away from the advancing waves.

'We'd better swim now if we're going to. The tide's coming in. Come on. We can dump our stuff up there.' He pointed to the rocks at the foot of the cliff and started to jog up the beach.

'Is it cold?' puffed Megan, following him.

'Freezing at first,' said Greg, swinging his rucksack off his back. 'But it's okay once you're in.'

'Is it cold?' mimicked Andy, from behind another rock. 'Don't be such a wimp.'

But Megan was the first changed and into the water. Determined not to make a fuss, she clamped her mouth shut and ran as far as she could into the waves and then plunged full length into the first breaker, gasping at the cold as the foam fizzled over her. She doggy paddled energetically to warm herself and then stood up, laughing at Andy's protests as he waded in. Greg pushed him under and then dived into a breaker and swam off at speed.

## Idwal's Bell

'Look at him go!' exclaimed Megan. 'I wish I could swim like that.'

'I expect we could if we swam every day,' growled Andy, wiping sea water out of his eyes and then crouching to keep his shoulders under water. 'We don't have the chance.'

'You spend too long glued to the X-Box anyway,' said Megan. 'You'll end up weak and flabby,' and without waiting to hear Andy's furious reply she swam away towards Greg and turned to look at the shore.

'Great, isn't it?' puffed Greg, surfacing next to her after a duck dive.

'Great beach,' said Megan. 'I love the waterfall.'

'It's much bigger after it's rained,' said Greg. 'Makes loads of spray when it lands on the rocks.'

'Is this beach dangerous?' asked Megan. 'We won't get cut off by the tide, will we?'

'S'pose you could in a storm and rising tide,' said Greg, 'but you'd have to be pretty careless. You can climb the cliffs in places and the cliff path is wide. You can walk up it three abreast. Easy peasy.'

Megan floated over a passing wave and stood again, the sea washing around her shoulders.

'The tide's quite strong,' she observed.

'Moving water always is,' said Greg. 'Not like a swimming pool. We don't get rips here, but when the tide's running out, a boat or an inflatable could soon be out at sea.'

Megan shivered. 'I don't know anything about tides,' she said. 'Only that they go in and out.'

'You would if you lived here,' Greg laughed. 'Lots of people here work by them. Anyone who uses a boat knows about tides.'

A passing wave picked Megan off her feet and dropped her a metre closer to the shore.

'What's it like when it's stormy?' she asked, turning towards Greg again.

'Very dangerous trying to bring a small boat in when the sea's rough,' said Greg, and duck dived again. He surfaced and shook his head. 'Big waves, strong current, poor visibility. Sometimes people in pleasure boats get caught in storms and the lifeboat has to go out and rescue them.'

Megan shivered again. She could imagine a small boat in a heaving sea, the rain pouring and the sky dark. Imagine the struggle to make the shore, and men throwing ropes against the wind.

# Idwal's Bell

Imagine running up the cliff path in the sluicing rain, trying to see if the people in the little boat had caught a rope so that they could be hauled ashore. Then hurrying down again, splashing and slipping through rivulets of rainwater. Cold hands, gripping the end of the rope and helping to pull, and pull, and pull…

Her fists were clenched again. She was gritting her teeth. Her heart was beating fast after the struggle to run in the wind and rain, yet here she was, playing in the sunglittered sea on a hot day, the broad safe beach in front of her and Andy wading towards her. Greg plunged downwards again and pulled Andy's feet from under him, leaving Andy yelling and splashing whilst Greg was up, blowing like a dolphin and laughing. Megan swam away, the fear fading, hands relaxing, and the summer gilding the day.

They spent half an hour in the shallow surf, diving over rollers and riding breakers before deciding they needed lunch.

They towelled briskly and climbed the cliff path with sand encrusted trainers and salty skin and arrived at the top of the cliff out of breath and hungry. A line of ponies and riders approached from the village path and walked in single file towards them past the bell tower.

'It's Alan Wetherton and his pony trekkers,' said Greg.

'Which one?' asked Andy.

'He's the one leading,' said Greg, pointing to a wiry fair-haired man on a tall bay horse. 'The one at the back is one of his helpers. They'll stop for lunch in a minute.'

'So that's the guy who doesn't want the monastery turned into a museum,' said Andy.

'That's mean,' said Megan. 'If he's making money from it, why shouldn't other people?'

'He says it'll destroy the peace and quiet,' Greg told her. 'But my Mum says that depends on how it's done. The museum itself doesn't have to be up here. It could be down in the village, and the monastery could just be preserved with information notices put up round it.'

'And he wouldn't have to bring drinks up if the riders could buy them in a tourist shop up here,' put in Andy.

They watched the ponies file past, and Alan Wetherton raised a hand to tell them all to halt. The helper from the back rode up the line telling all the riders to dismount and take their lunches from the canvas bags strapped to the saddles.

## Idwal's Bell

Greg walked across to them and stroked one of the ponies. The rider, a boy, smiled at him and Andy and Megan could see Greg looking at the saddle, when Alan Wetherton trotted up to Greg and shouted.

'What do you think you're doing?'
Greg sprang backwards, startled. 'I was only looking at the saddle,' he protested.

'It's none of your business,' said Alan Wetherton, and he made an angry gesture with one arm. 'Clear off!'

'I'm sorry,' said Greg. 'I wasn't doing anything.'

'The ponies don't like strangers round them,' said Alan Wetherton. 'You might have been kicked.'

'He doesn't look like kicking,' muttered Greg. 'He looks half asleep.'

'Clear off!' shouted Alan Wetherton. 'And don't come back!'

Greg gave him a long hard stare and walked slowly back to Andy and Megan.

'What was all that about?' asked Andy.

Greg shrugged. 'I don't know, 'he said. 'I was just talking to that boy when Witherguts came up and started shouting at me to clear off. Funny guy.'

## Picnic

They watched in silence as the ponies were led through an archway.

'That's the way to the old kitchen,' said Greg. 'I expect they're going to get their drink.'

'I could do with a drink,' said Andy. 'Let's have our picnic. Where shall we go?'

'Let's see where they go first,' said Megan.

'Why?' said Greg. 'We're allowed up here. He can't really tell us to clear off.'

'He seemed pretty positive about it,' said Andy.

'But he can't,' insisted Greg. 'Anyone can come up here. I'm going to sit where he can see us and watch him.'

'You'll only annoy him,' warned Megan.

'Tough,' said Greg. 'I'll stay away from the ponies, but we don't have to go away. No one's ever told me to clear off before. And I'm not going to!'

'Maybe he just meant leave the saddles alone,' said Andy, as they crossed the grass behind the monastery to a clump of wind stunted oak trees.

'Why? What's he on about? He's mad.' Greg flung himself on the ground under the trees, scowling. The trekkers were unsaddling the ponies and the helper was carrying the saddles away to somewhere out of sight behind a wall.

'Looks like he's putting them in the old kitchen,' said Greg, unpacking his sandwiches. 'Why don't they just put them on the ground?'

'I thought there'd be more ponies than that,' said Andy, already chewing.

'There are seven, plus the two horses,' said Megan, pulling her sketch pad out of her rucksack, and searching for a pencil.

'The helper's disappeared now,' said Andy as the trekkers settled down to eat in the shade of one of the ruined walls.

'Perhaps he's taking some of the ponies to get water,' said Megan, sketching busily.

'Let's have a look,' said Greg, leaning towards her. 'Cool! That's really good. Do you do a lot?'

'She's at it all the time,' said Andy, biting into his second sandwich. 'Her room disappears under millions of sketches and paintings. You'd better look out. She'll draw you when you're not looking.'

'You'll be famous one day,' said Greg. 'But most artists don't get famous till they're dead.'

'Yeah,' agreed Andy. 'They starve all their lives, painting pictures nobody wants till they come into fashion a hundred years later.'

'Thanks very much!' said Megan, throwing her pencil at Andy. He picked it up and so she shut her sketch book and started on her lunch.

'How many treks a week?' she asked Greg.

'Dunno. I've never counted. They trek from Witherguts' place to the cliff path on the other side of the river, down into the village and up here. Then I think they go through those woods into the hills.'

'Be stiff the next day if you weren't used to it,' said Andy, searching his picnic bag for a chocolate biscuit.

Megan retrieved her pencil and Greg bit into a peach. 'Do you have extra drawing lessons?' he asked.

'No.'

'You're really good.' Greg leaned over to look at her sketch again. 'Are you good at painting too?' Megan wrinkled up her nose. 'No. I've been saving up for a good paint box. I tried to win one at the school fete on Saturday, but I didn't.' She sighed.

'Should've put the money towards a paint box instead,' said Greg, wagging a finger.

'She ended up going to a fortune teller of all things,' said Andy. 'Anyway, I'm going to snooze,' and he stretched out on the grass.

'Well, you made me!' retorted Megan, throwing a tuft of grass at him.

'Cool! What did she say?' asked Greg.

'A load of rubbish,' said Andy, before Megan could reply. 'I could have done better.'

'No, you couldn't,' argued Megan. 'She told me I was going on a journey towards water soon and here we are.'

'That was chance!' Andy smirked. 'It's the sort of thing they all say.'

'That's not what you said Saturday night!'

'It was though,' said Andy. 'What else did she tell you that was true?'

'How do I know? It hasn't happened yet. Anyway, it was scary.' Megan carefully smudged a pencil line with one finger.

'Scary!' scoffed Andy. 'You're scared of your own shadow!'

'What was scary?' asked Greg alert, like a terrier after a rat.

Megan was silent. She didn't want to tell them about the face in the crystal ball. She had begun to think she'd imagined it, but those blue eyes haunted her.

'It was weird,' she said at last, bending over her sketch so that her red curls hid her face.

'But what did she tell you?' persisted Greg.

'She said something about something really old. Something round, but sharp. And a shadow.'

'Which one?' asked Andy. 'The sun's shining. There are shadows everywhere.'

'She said a shadow from the past. And something about living water. She didn't understand that.'

'Well nor do I,' said Andy. 'It's all rubbish.'

'I do,' said Greg at once, his eyes round behind his spectacles. 'What about the waterfall?'

'What do you mean?' asked Megan, turning to look at him.

'It's fresh water,' said Greg. 'And it's moving like it's living.'

'Yeah. So does rain,' scoffed Andy.'

'Well you never know,' said Greg. 'It's the water the monks lived on. It'll be fun to see if any more comes true.'

'How're you going to know which shadow's which?' pointed out Andy. 'You can't go around asking them if they're old.'

'I said she didn't mean a shadow made by something blocking the sun,' said Megan.

'What then?'

'A bad happening,' suggested Greg, bloodthirstily swiping his fore finger across his throat. 'Something like that.'

'Or a ghost?' Greg raised his hands and wriggled his fingers.

Megan glanced at him again, feeling goosebumps rising on her arms again. 'I don't know,' she lied as her heart beat faster.

'No such thing as ghosts,' retorted Andy.

'Megan looks like one now,' said Greg. 'She's gone all white.'

'I don't!' Megan protested. 'And I don't want to see a ghost.' She bit into a sandwich but found she didn't want to eat it.

Andy sat up. 'Look. The riders are getting ready to go.'

They watched the trekkers leading their ponies back through the kitchen garden, to reappear a few minutes later having saddled up.

'There's the helper,' observed Andy. 'Where was he while they had their lunch?'

'Perhaps he guards the saddles and saddle bags,' suggested Megan.

'In the old kitchen, I expect,' said Greg. 'That's where they store the drinks.'

'We could go and see when they've gone,' said Andy

They packed their rucksacks while they watched the riders mount. Alan Wetherton placed himself at the head of the line and the helper brought up the rear.

## Picnic

When all was ready the trekkers rode in single file from the monastery, heading towards a path through the trees.

'C'mon,' said Andy. 'Let's go and look.'

They crossed the grassy clifftop to the ancient archway which marked the edge of the garden, passing under it in silence, over awed by the age of the building. Before them stretched a large flat area surrounded by ruined walls which had sheltered the kitchen garden for centuries. The narrow, clear ribbon of water chattered through it, and three or four metres from the archway, plunged underground.

Megan walked curiously towards it, stooped and held her fingers in the cold, strong current, finding herself wondering how many people had done the same before her. How many monks, she wondered, must have cupped their hands to drink the water while working in the kitchen gardens? She could almost see them round her now…

They took the path made by the ponies to the kitchen wall. There was no doorway there, so they followed the wall round to the seaward side. Here were the ruined walls of the other parts of the monastery, some barely existent, but some intact, rearing up into the blue sky, defiant of time and weather.

# Idwal's Bell

The refectory and the kitchen were almost whole. A doorway with no door led into the refectory which still had stone columns that once supported the roof. A seagull perched on one of these, neck stretched, calling loudly into the summer breeze, while his companions glided around the ruins on the air currents rising up the cliffs. At the seaward end of the refectory was a huge fireplace, large enough to stand in. Andy walked down to it and looked up into the chimney.

'You can just see daylight,' he said, 'but the chimney's not straight.'

'Good thing, or the rain would put out the fire,' said Greg. 'C'mon! Let's have a look at the kitchen.'

He walked to the landward end of the refectory where a large wooden door separated it from the kitchen. He grasped the metal ring and twisted it, but the door didn't move.

'It's locked!' he said, startled.

'I guess it has to be,' said Andy coming up. 'If Alan Wetherton stores the riders' drinks in there, he wouldn't want other picnickers taking them.'

'I suppose he's got special permission,' Greg said, 'but I didn't think anyone could use the monastery like that.' Frowning, he tried the door again, but it wouldn't budge.

There was a large keyhole underneath the iron ring, but no key. 'I'm going to see if there's another way in.'

Andy and Megan followed him out of the refectory, and back into the kitchen garden. They walked right round the kitchen, but there was no other entrance.

'I suppose that's where they put the saddles too,' said Megan. 'They lock them in there with the saddle bags while the riders have their lunch.'

'So where did the helper go?' asked Andy.

'Maybe he sits in here with them in case someone needs to get something from their saddle-bag or wants another drink,' suggested Greg.

'So why can't they have the saddles outside somewhere?' Andy queried. 'It's crazy. Why does he sit in here on his own?'

'He can't really do that,' protested Megan. 'Maybe he cleans the saddles or something.'

'Not enough time,' said Andy. 'Weird.'

'I wish we could get in there,' said Greg. He frowned, his eyebrows beetling behind his spectacles.

'I expect there's a chimney,' said Megan. Greg stared at her. 'Of course there is! We could climb down the chimney!'

## Idwal's Bell

They left the locked door and ran round into the kitchen garden away from the building until, looking back they could identify a short chimney stack rising from the kitchen region.

'There is a chimney!  Great!  All we need is a decent rope!' whooped Greg.

'If we can get up there, we may not need to go down the chimney,' said Andy.  'The refectory roof has gone.  May be this one has too.'

'Still better to have a rope,' said Greg, already searching the ancient wall for footholds.

'Someone's coming,' said Megan, looking towards the garden archway, as a family of four appeared, looking at the monastery.

'Shucks!' said Greg, disappointed.  'We'll have to wait.'

'Tomorrow,' said Andy.

# Chapter Seven
## Eavesdropping
### AD 994

Gylan and Margiad crouched by the doorpost of the hut, as close as they could to the doorway without being seen from inside. The sky was darkening and Gylan knew his mother would soon return. He hoped he would see her before she saw him, so though his ears listened to the conversation inside the hut, his eyes watched the path Rhiannon would take through the village on her way home.

'I doubt if you'll persuade them to do it,' Gyffes, Gylan's father was saying. 'It's a lot of work for what many of them think is no purpose.'

Idwal crashed his fist down on the rough wooden bench that stood between them. 'It does have purpose,' he argued. 'It will slow them down! Give the village a few more vital minutes to prepare.'

'I know, I know,' agreed Gyffes, interlacing his fingers and pressing his palms together. He pulled out his knife and began to sharpen it on the stone that lay on the bench. 'Though thank God we haven't seen them for thirteen years now.'

Gylan counted on his fingers. *Thirteen years? A year before I was born.*

Silently he mouthed to Margiad, 'They're talking about the raiders,' and she nodded.

'Every year brings us closer to their coming again,' insisted Idwal, and Margiad nudged Gylan in the back. This time it was he who nodded.

'They haven't come near us in that time.' The silvery scrape of blade on stone increased.

'But we know they're not far away,' pointed out Idwal. 'Ireland? No distance to them.'

'Perhaps they're content there.' Scrape, scrape, scrape. Gylan imagined the blade flashing in the light from the fire, and wished he had a knife.

Then he remembered he'd left his staff in the forest by the cattle pen. He must make a new one, before his father noticed.

'We know they aren't. And there's vengeance.'

Gylan edged closer, concentrating, and Margiad wriggled up behind him.

### Eavesdropping

'I know what you're thinking. But you can't be sure,' Gyffes was saying, sticking his knife into the top of the bench, and pulling it out again, making an indented pattern in the wood.

*Sure of what?* Wondered Gylan, straining his eyes to see through the deepening dusk. Was that his mother just past Cadoc's house?

'I'm sure.'

It was his mother, leading his little sister, Rhianna, by the hand. He saw her wave to Cadoc's wife as she passed, walking towards her own home, her woollen cloak rippling about her. Gylan stood, anxious to appear as though he had just arrived, but through stooping so long, one foot had become numb, and he lost his balance and fell into the hut, sprawling at his father's feet.

Gyffes shot out a hand and hauled him up.

'What are you doing? Where have you been?'

Then, noticing Gylan rubbing his tingling foot, and Margiad hesitating in the doorway, 'Have you been listening? Have you?' He shook Gylan roughly. 'Answer me!'

'Yes,' said Gylan boldly, as his mother entered the hut. 'I was listening because I want to know. I've often asked you and Mahme about the raiders, but you won't tell me anything.'

'Oh Gylan,' protested his mother, undoing Rhianna's cloak. 'You don't need to know about it, and nor does Margiad.'

'But I do!' shouted Gylan. 'How can I be prepared if I don't know what's going to happen? I'm not a baby anymore. And I'm not afraid of nightmares.'

'Enough!' growled Gyffes, shaking him. 'When we think you're old enough, we'll tell you.'

Gylan looked down, but muttered, 'I'm old enough now! I can help. I help with the goats, and with cutting wood. If I'm old enough to do that I'm old enough to know about the raiders.'

Both Gyffes and Idwal laughed, but Rhiannon looked worried. She pushed Rhianna out the door, saying, 'Go and play with Eseld. You needn't know,' she repeated, turning to Gylan and Margiad.

## Eavesdropping

'They won't come again.'

Gylan lifted his head. 'But Idwal thinks they will,' he said. He turned to his uncle. 'Don't you? That's why the monastery is there isn't it? And the bell tower. That's why the monks keep watch above the waterfall. I know. I've seen them.'

There was a brief silence, then Idwal said, 'It's true we hope God will keep us safe. We pray for our safety every day. But I believe God helps those who help themselves. What did you hear, Gylan?'

Gylan lifted his chin. 'I heard you say you wanted to build some huts up behind the cliffs before the monastery,' he said, 'but I didn't hear why.'

'You shouldn't have been listening' snapped Gyffes. 'Sneaks listen at doorways and I don't want a sneak for a son!'

'I'm not a sneak,' answered Gylan, anger flaring in his face. 'I want to help!'

'That's a sneak's way of going about it!'

'How else can I go about it if you won't tell me anything!'

This time it was Gyffes's fist that crashed on to the table. 'Don't answer me like that!' he roared, and Gylan blenched.

'I'm sorry,' he muttered, then looked his father in the face and said, 'But I want to know what to do if they come again.'

# Idwal's Bell

Margiad twisted round to face Rhiannon. 'I know about it!' she cried, pointing at her chest. 'Eywy screams at night.'

'What's that on your wrist?' demanded Gyffes, grasping her hand. 'Violets! Have you two been in the forest? Have you no sense? You know you shouldn't go there.'

'Oooh no! We only go there when the raiders come,' said Gylan sarcastically. 'We found the cattle pen. But I'm not going to hide in there. I'm going to fight!'

'Who told you about that?' wailed his mother. 'I didn't want you to know about that yet!'

'Hush, Rhiannon,' grumbled Gyffes. 'What's done is done, though I didn't want him to know just yet. Another year, I thought.'

Gylan's fists clenched as he faced his father. 'I need to know what to do,' he repeated. 'Margiad said I wouldn't know what to do, and she's right. Why don't you tell us?'

'Margiad, how much have you been told by your Mahme?' asked Idwal, his blue eyes watching her intently. Margiad looked down, and then looked back up at him, tracing the scar with her own eyes. Idwal smiled again.

# Eavesdropping

'I hear Eywy screaming at night. I heard Mahme telling her about the cattle pen where we can take the animals and hide. But I won't go in that cattle pen, even if there's room.' She shook her head, and Gylan glanced at her and nodded.

Idwal nodded, still smiling. 'Why not?' he asked.

'If they found us, we'd be trapped,' said Gylan, and heard his mother gasp.

'Holy Mother! It's either the raiders or wolves,' she whispered.

'Which is why we must do everything to stop the raiders ever reaching the forest,' said Idwal, flattening his hand on the bench. 'We must defeat them here. The bell will bring them in to Monastery Bay. They'll raid the monastery, then the empty homes, and by then the village will be prepared.'

'Empty homes?' exclaimed Rhiannon. 'Is that what we must build now?'

'Yes,' said Idwal, clenching his hand into a fist. 'We must.'

'I see we must,' agreed Gyffes, digging a small chunk of wood out of the bench top with his knife. 'But most of us won't want to spare the time.'

## Idwal's Bell

'We will,' said Gylan. 'Won't we Margiad?'

Margiad nodded. 'Will the brothers in the monastery help?' she asked Idwal.

'Yes,' said Idwal. 'We'll all help. And we'll do it soon.'

Rhiannon put her arms round the children. 'We can all help,' she said, 'but they won't come again. Pray that they won't come again.'

Up on the cliff, the monastery bell began to chime, echoing out in the dusk, calling the monks to evening prayer.

'Vespers,' said Idwal. 'I must go.' He stood up and nodded to them. 'Peace be with you all.'

'Peace be with you Idwal,' they murmured, as he ducked out of the hut and strode towards the gate in the fortifications that led to the little monastery crouching beyond the tall bell tower, overlooking the quiet sea.

# Chapter Eight
## The Bell At Night

The rope was in her hands, and she was hauling it downwards again and again while the bell rang wildly with every pull. Heart thudding and chest heaving, she pulled and pulled, and the bell tolled ever more loudly until her throat rasped and her hands bled, and she could stand the pain and the clangour no longer

'Help me! Help!' she cried, fighting with something that was holding her down. 'Help me! Help!' Then she crumpled sideways, rolling on to the floor, tangled in her quilt and tugging at her under sheet, as the bell still pounded in her ears.

'Andy! Andy! The bell! Quick! Can you hear it? The bell's ringing!' Megan crawled across the floor to the door still calling. 'Andy! Andy! Quick! The bell's ringing!'

## Idwal's Bell

She reached up for the door handle as Andy pushed her door from the other side.

'Megs! Shut up! What on earth's the matter?'

'The bell! It won't stop ringing! It's louder this time! Can't you hear it?' Megan struggled to her feet.

Andy tilted his head on one side to listen. 'No, I can't,' he said. 'Can't hear a thing! You're mad!'

Megan listened. She could hear nothing.

'But it woke me up,' she insisted. 'It did! It kept ringing and ringing and ringing!'

'You were dreaming,' said Andy.

Megan put her hands over her ears and shook her head. 'I told myself that this morning, but when Auntie Liz said about the wind off the sea, I thought it was the wind ringing the bell.'

Andy frowned. 'It could have been,' he said, and turned and crossed the landing and went down the three steps to the window that looked across the garden to the clifftop.

'Was it windy this morning? I can't remember. It isn't windy now. It's as calm and clear as anything, with a moon.'

Megan shuddered. 'I was so scared,' she said.

Her curls were tangled and her eyes wide with fear.

Come and look,' said Andy. 'Then p'raps you'll believe me!'

Megan followed him and looked out. The bell tower stood stark against the starry sky. There was no movement and no sound.

Megan shuddered again. 'I did hear it,' she said. 'I'm certain. Even if I can't hear it now.'

'Okay,' said Andy. 'Let's go and look.'

'We can't! How?'

'Easy peasy. Down the fire escape.' Megan glanced round.

'What's the time?'

Andy shrugged and went to fetch his watch. He came back doing it up on his wrist. 'It's one thirty,' he said. 'I bet everyone's asleep. That is if you didn't wake them with your yelling. Come on. Get dressed and we'll go and have a look.'

'We can't go out now!'

''Course we can, Scaredy cat. Who's to know? We can go up and listen to see if the bell does ring in the wind, and if there's no wind, we'll see what's ringing it. If it did ring at all.'

'It did!'

'Okay. Let's look.'

'Supposing someone sees us?'

'Who's going to see us at this time of night? And we won't be long. It's not far. Put on something dark that won't show up.'

## Idwal's Bell

In a few minutes they were on the landing again dressed in jeans and sweaters and opening the window to the fire escape. In seconds they were outside on a metal stairway that went down to the rose-scented garden. They crept past the window on the floor below, their trainers making no sound on the steps. There was no sign of anyone else being awake. Soon they were on the ground and running across the back lawn to the vegetable patch. The moon left inky shadows behind the runner bean row and a breeze rustled against the currant bushes, but there was no sound from the bell. A laurel hedge grew along the post and rail fence, but they pushed through the branches on to the rails and jumped from the top, Then they were pounding up the grassy track to the moonlit monastery ruins on the top of the cliff.

As they reached the crest of the rise, Megan pulled Andy to a halt.

'Wait,' she hissed. 'Supposing there's someone in there? We don't want them to know we're here.'

'Why not?' asked Andy. 'They can't go ring-ing the bell in the middle of the night and expect people not to notice.'

'I know, but it may be vandals or something.'

'Okay. We'll hide behind the kitchen garden wall and watch for a bit.' He glanced over his shoulder at the ruins and then looked back at the ancient tower. 'But I want to listen at the bell tower first.'

'I'm sure I heard it. I did. I know I did,' insisted Megan, and shivered as she remembered the wild clangour.

The bell tower rose out of a small house like structure at its base. There was a doorway to this but most of the roof had gone. Andy and Megan didn't dare go inside, so they crouched down outside and waited for a breeze. It soon came, cooling their cheeks and lifting their hair, but though they could hear the waves whispering on the beach below and the waterfall splashing busily far to their right, no sound came from the tower above them.

'Well, it isn't ringing now,' said Andy. 'You must've been dreaming. Come on. We'd better go back.'

Megan followed him across the cliff top towards the path, and then cannoned into him when he stopped and turned.

'What?'

'Sh!'

She followed his gaze to where the silvery light glimmered on the wrinkling sea.

'What is it?' she whispered.

'I thought I heard something.' He set off up the path to the cliff top.

'What sort of thing? The waves?' asked Megan, following him.

'No. A creaking.'

'Now you're dreaming.'

'I'm not! Get down!' Andy snapped, dragging at her sleeve. 'We must be on the skyline.'

They flattened themselves face down on the grass. Megan could feel her heart thudding again and a storm of panic welled up inside her.

'Can you see anything?' Andy muttered.

Megan looked up and peered out to sea. Its calm surface reflected the light of the full moon, revealing the black bulk of Gull Island. She strained her eyes, searching the watery expanse. 'There's a boat!' she said.

'Where?'

'Just beyond the island. Look! To the left.'

'Oh yes! Looks like a motorboat. But that wouldn't make a creaking. I heard it again then. Listen!'

Megan closed her eyes and concentrated. Then she heard it too, a regular creak…creak… creak.

'It's close. To our left.'

# The Bell at Night

'Coming closer,' whispered Andy. 'C'mon. Keep down till we're away from the cliff.'

But Megan eased closer to the edge, clutching the damp grass. The cliff fell away and the sea crawled beneath her. Her head reeled.

'Megs! Come back!'

'Shhh!' She peered again into the darkness.

The creaking stopped. At the water's edge, some way from the cliff, she could make out a figure hauling a rowing boat up the sand.

'Someone's coming ashore! Look!'

Andy wriggled to her side and looked where she pointed. The figure, dark against the gleaming sand, picked something heavy out of the boat and came striding up the beach.

'Quick!'

# Idwal's Bell

They slid backwards, and when they were sure they could no longer be seen against the sky, turned and fled towards the monastery, round the kitchen and into the refectory where they crouched panting in the shadow of a rubbled wall. For a few moments all they could hear was the waterfall in its unending tumble beyond the ruins, but then heavy footsteps thudded across the grass towards them. They huddled lower, hard against the stones, ducking their heads. Andy gripped his elbows and held his breath and Megan sunk her teeth into her knuckles.

The footsteps came closer, right into the refectory, and stopped. Megan's heart pounded in the silence and then there was a thud, as if something heavy had been dropped. A key scraped in a lock, a latch lifted and there was a long creaking sound as the door to the old kitchen was pushed open. Andy raised his head a little to look over the broken wall. He could make out a man picking up a wide flat shape and going into the kitchen. Behind him, Megan made neither sound nor movement. Her legs ached. Her feet were numb. They waited and waited. Nothing.

'He's gone in the kitchen,' whispered Andy. 'He's got a key.'

'How many people have keys?'

'Don't know. Greg might.'

There was a jangling tune of a mobile phone and an exclamation of annoyance. They heard a terse, 'Yes?' from the man, but then only unintelligible murmurings, muffled by the kitchen walls.

'Can we go back now?' pleaded Megan.

'No. If he comes out, he'll see us.'

Minutes ticked past. Andy swayed with fatigue and propped himself more firmly against the wall. Megan closed her eyes. Her spine began to prickle. Below, the sea murmured rhythmically, like someone breathing, and the image in the crystal ball swam before her. She curled up tighter, trying to make the scarred face disappear, but blood oozed from the base of the scar and trickled down the cheek and chin. She gasped.

'Shush Megs,' muttered Andy, still looking ahead.

Megan buried her face in her hands, trembling with fear.

Andy turned to look. 'Don't be silly,' he hissed. He turned back again.

# Idwal's Bell

She wanted to weep and cry out, but when at last the vision faded and she dared to open her eyes there was just the grass and the ruins, standing as they had for centuries under the star scattered sky. She swallowed and clutched the weathered stones and then rocked back to sit on the cold grass, resting her head on her knees, with a sob of relief as her heart still pounded.

'Sit still Megs!'

'I saw something,' she whispered.

'Shut up, you idiot!' hissed Andy.

'Oh shut up yourself!' muttered Megan, rocking backwards and forwards, fighting for calm.

Then, 'What's that smell?'

Andy sniffed. 'Smoke. He's burning something.'

'What?' She could hear the panic in her own voice.

'How do I know? Let's get further back, in case he comes out.'

They wormed their way backwards along the wall just as they heard the man coming out of the kitchen. He pulled the door to and locked it and they heard footsteps leaving the refectory and padding across the grass back to the cliff path.

As still as the stones around them, they crouched in the shadow of the ancient wall while the moon smiled down into the refectory. Minutes later, Andy straightened up.

'Do you think he's gone back to the boat?' asked Megan, looking round. The monastery stood pale and still.

'Let's go and see.'

Andy flitted up to the cliff top and Megan could only stumble after him, her legs still weak and trembling. When they neared the edge, they dropped to all fours. The rowing boat had gone from the beach.

They stared into the dark, and a while later they heard the distant engine of the bigger boat splutter into life.

In silence, they watched the motorboat, with the skiff tethered behind her, crossing the silver water until it disappeared behind the headland into St. Idwal's, and they could hear it no more.

'That was Alan Wetherton, night fishing round Gull Island,' said Megan, sitting back on her heels and running her hands through her hair.

'Funny time to bring drinks up to the kitchen though,' said Andy.

'Weird,' croaked Megan, rubbing her legs to try to stop them shaking. 'Especially as Auntie Liz said he went up in his Range Rover on Sunday, and we know he only used nine drinks yesterday.'

'Really weird,' agreed Andy. 'We'd better get back.' And they hurried across the grass towards the path down to the house, Megan looking behind every few paces. As they walked down the slope, she turned one last time, but she could only see the bell tower, pointing mutely into the night sky.

## Chapter Nine
### Down The Kitchen
### Chimney

Greg arrived the next morning carrying a large overnight bag, while Andy and Megan were eating breakfast.

'Is it all right for me to come again?' he asked, turning his bespectacled gaze upon Auntie Liz. 'I thought I could help and then we could have another picnic lunch, like yesterday.'

'Of course it is,' said Auntie Liz, eyeing the bag. 'Have you come to stay?'

Greg's eyes widened. 'It's just my swimming gear,' he said, 'and my football, and my lunch.'

'Big football,' said Mum, 'or is it a big lunch?'

'Both,' grinned Greg.

'Have some orange juice while Megan and Andy finish their toast,' offered Auntie Liz. 'Or would you like some toast too?'

'Yes please,' said Greg, and sat at the table next to Andy. 'What do you have to do today?' he asked.

'I don't know,' Andy replied.

'Open the greenhouse please, 'said Auntie Liz, 'and pick any ripe tomatoes. Then pick any more ripe black currants and any decent sized runner beans. It won't take long.'

She was right. By eleven o'clock they were back in the house to collect their swimming gear and another picnic lunch. Andy and Megan stowed their goods into a rucksack, but Greg refused the offer of a smaller bag for his stuff. They puffed up the track, but when they reached the crest of the cliffs Andy said, 'Quick! We've got something to tell you.'

He ran towards the oak trees, and sat in the shade, followed by Megan and Greg.

'What is it?' panted Greg, throwing down his bag and sitting on it. Andy told him about the night's adventures, with Megan filling in details.

Greg whistled. 'Stinking Sturgeon! And you think it was Witherguts?'

'It must have been. He had a key. Does anyone else have a key?'

'Shouldn't think so. Mighty peculiar.'

'What?' asked Andy, raising one eyebrow.

'I said it's mighty peculiar,' said Greg. 'Why bring extra drinks in the middle of the night: And what was he burning?'

'He could've been burning empty cartons,' put in Megan. 'If he comes up today with a huge party of trekkers, we'll know why he needed so many drinks.'

'Yeah. We'll wait and watch,' agreed Greg, 'but it doesn't explain why the helper disappeared during the picnic.'

'There's something else we don't know,' said Megan.

'What?'

'Who rang the bell, of course!'

Both boys stared at her.

'You imagined it!' said Andy, shaking his head and spreading his hands.

'I didn't!' insisted Megan. 'It woke me yesterday morning and again last night. Otherwise we wouldn't have come up here last night, would we?'

'True,' admitted Andy. 'But you keep being spooked and I've never heard or seen anything.'

'Well, I did!' insisted Megan.

'Maybe it's the wind,' suggested Greg tactfully, looking from one to the other, but Andy shook his head.

'We stood by the tower and listened when the breeze blew and there's not a sound,' he said.

'It sounded really desperate,' said Megan. 'Like someone trapped inside.'

They all stared at each other and then leapt to their feet and ran across the grass to the bell tower.

'Didn't you go inside last night?' puffed Greg.

'No,' said Megan. 'I was afraid it was vandals, and then Andy heard the oars creak, so we looked and saw the boat.'

'Megs, you must have dreamt it,' persuaded Andy, but Megan shook her head.

'I didn't,' she said again. 'I know I didn't,' and she hammered on the wooden door. It didn't budge and there was no sound from inside.

They crept round to the broken down entrance of the little shelter at the foot of the tower and Greg stepped into the shadowed doorway and stopped. 'Well, that's strange!' he said.

'What?' Megan and Andy pushed forward.

The stone shelter was empty. A wooden door shut off the entrance to the tower steps and on it was a large white notice printed with red letters:

DANGER!
BUILDING  UNSAFE
KEEP  OUT

# Down The Kitchen Chimney

'This is a terrific mystery,' said Greg, pleased. 'I've always wanted to solve a mystery. First we have to get into that kitchen.'

'How?' asked Andy.

'Like we said yesterday. Down the chimney.'

Greg's eyes gleamed. 'I've brought a rope! C'mon! Before Witherguts gets here with his troupe!'

They tore back to the oak trees and Greg unzipped his bag and pulled out a coil of blue nylon rope. Tangled in it were his phone, his lunch, a torch and a partly crushed tube of Smarties.

'See?' he said, brandishing the rope and picking out his other belongings. 'It's light, but it's ever so strong. All we need is a good piece of wood to go across the top of the chimney so we can tie the rope to it. I can do a safe knot. There might something in these trees.' He stuffed the phone, the Smarties and his lunch back into the bag next to the football and zipped it up again.

They split up to search under the oak trees but all they had found was rotten branches lying amongst the brambles, when Andy came across a fence, dividing the trees from a field of sheep. Some fence posts had been replaced and a strong stake lay abandoned next to a roll of sheep netting.

'That's exactly what we need,' said Greg when he saw it. 'C'mon.'

They ran back to their bags, and picking up the rope, jogged across to the monastery kitchen garden, Greg dragging the heavy post behind them.

'Anyone about?' asked Andy, surveying the cliff top.

'There was someone walking a dog earlier,' said Megan, 'but they've gone now.'

'Right,' said Greg. 'How do we get up to the kitchen chimney?'

They followed the kitchen wall around to the right until they could see the kitchen chimney above them. A little further on, the wall was broken and rough, with gaps in the mortar.

'Great,' said Andy. 'We can climb up there. Watch out for loose stones.'

'Can you climb?' Greg asked Megan and Andy.

''Course we can!' retorted Andy.

'I've climbed the apple tree at home,' said Megan. 'I've never tried to climb a wall.'

'Well, now's your chance,' said Andy. 'Who's going first?'

'I am,' said Greg, securing one end of the rope round his middle. 'I climb the cliffs. You tie the stake to the other end and I'll pull it up.' And without a backward glance, he put a foot in a niche in the wall and eased himself upwards.

Andy and Megan watched as he climbed higher, but he didn't falter. At the top, he turned and grinned triumphantly down at them from his perch next to the old kitchen chimney.

'Easy peasy,' he called. 'Come on!'

'Okay!' called Andy, tying the stake to the end of the rope. He waved to Greg, who hauled up the stake and lodged it next to him. Andy and Megan could see him retying the knot and placing the stake across the chimney opening.

'Is it long enough?' called Megan.

'Easily.'

'Okay. We're coming up.' Andy pushed Megan towards the wall. 'Go on Megs,' he said. 'If you fall, I'll catch you.'

'I'm not going to fall,' snapped Megan.

'Well go on then. The riders'll be here soon. We should've waited till they'd gone.'

'They may not come today,' said Megan, putting her foot in the niche Greg had found.

'Just concentrate, will you?' muttered Andy, giving her a helping shove.

'Just concentrate, will you?' muttered Andy, giving her a helping shove.

There were footholds where stones had fallen away, and tough grass grew in some of the cracks offering secure hand holds. Minutes later all three of them stood on the top of the old kitchen next to the short chimney stack, looking down on the corrugated iron roof that covered the kitchen.

'So he's covered it in as well as locked the door,' said Andy.

'Looks like it,' said Greg. He prodded the metal with his foot. 'Good strong roof.'

Megan looked towards the sea, wishing she had carried up her sketch pad. She would have enjoyed drawing the skeletal arches of the refectory, still a little higher than they were, framing Gull Island in the middle distance. High on the refectory chimney a large herring gull eyed them, before reaching forwards and calling loudly across the ruin, and two jackdaws on the kitchen garden wall below rolled turquoise eyes disapprovingly up at them.

Greg fed the rope down the chimney.

'Who's going down?' asked Megan. 'It looks really dark down there.'

'There'll be light from the chimney,' said Greg. 'You can see the floor of the fireplace if you look down, and I've got a torch.'

## Down The Kitchen Chimney

'Be careful!' snapped Andy, as Megan leaned over the chimney shaft to see.

'All right, all right! I'm only looking.'

'Shut up, you two. I'm going down. I've tied some knots so I can grip, but I'm going to sort of abseil. You'll have to pull me up if I can't climb up.'

'I'll go down,' said Andy, and Megan smiled to herself, thinking he was feeling responsible.

'No,' said Greg. 'I'm lighter than you. I'll be easier to pull up.' He passed the rope around his back, grasped it with his right hand, and sat on the chimney with his feet dangling down inside.

'Whoo! It's a weird feeling,' he chuckled. 'My stomach just turned over. Okay. Here I go.'

'Be careful,' urged Megan, but Greg grinned at her and lowered himself into the hole. Megan and Andy held the ends of the stake to make sure it didn't slip. The knot around it tightened as Greg descended, and they could hear his trainers scraping against the sides of the chimney.

'He's okay,' said Andy. 'It's not too far down.'

The top of Greg's fair head grew smaller and smaller, but when they thought it would disappear into the blackness, it stopped.

'Are you okay?' Megan called.

'Yup! I'm here!' Came a muffled voice from below.

'What can you see?' called Andy.

'Nothing, at the moment. Hang on. I'll get out my torch.'

Andy and Megan waited at the top, peering into the darkness. Greg's head disappeared. The seagull chided them raucously again.

'Good thing we put suntan stuff on,' observed Megan. 'We'd be cooked up here.'

'Can you see anything yet?' Andy called.

'Not much. Hold on. I think I've found the drinks.'

Megan leaned over the shaft. She could see Greg's torchlight flashing occasionally and hear the rustle of thin plastic. There was a silence, broken by a swishing sound and then some muttering.

## Down The Kitchen Chimney

The torchlight was turned on the rest of the kitchen and held there for a few moments, before sweeping back towards the fireplace again. There were fumbling sounds, a scraping, and then a loud, metallic crash and a clatter.

'Greg!' yelled Andy. 'Greg! Are you okay?'

There was a scrabbling sound and some more scraping.

'Yeah. It's okay. Just an oven door. I opened the oven.'

'Is it broken?' called Andy.

'No. It comes right out. I've got to put it back otherwise they'll know someone's been in here.'

Megan and Andy could hear him grunt as he picked up the door, a crunch as he rested it on the floor, and another grunt and more scraping as he put it back where it belonged.

Megan turned round, and gasped. She grabbed Andy's arm and pointed.

'There are more drinks in the oven,' Greg shouted up the shaft. 'I'll put the door back and come up. Andy? Can you hear me?'

Andy leant over the chimney and hissed, 'Greg! Hurry up! The riders are coming!'

# Chapter Ten
## Storm
### AD 994

Gylan prised another large stone from under a bed of seaweed and stowed it into his sling, which lay flat on the pebbled sand. Behind him the grey waves crashed onto the beach, the spray wetting his tunic and salting his lips. Large raindrops began to patter singly around him and then sluiced in a deluge, sticking his hair to his face and pounding his body. Above the whistling and roaring he heard a shout, and the onshore wind whipped into his eyes as he tried to look up. Through the downpour he could make out a figure waving on the cliff top. The arms beckoned in a huge gesture, and Gylan gathered up the ends of his sling and heaved up his load.

'Margiad!' he yelled. She was to his left, bending over a big stone, pulling it from its bed, her red hair darkened to auburn by the rain, and her bare feet pink with the salt and the cold.

# Storm

'Margiad! They're calling us up!' She turned towards him and looked where he pointed. She waved in answer, and she too picked up the corners of her sling, banging it against her legs as she stumbled up the beach.

Several of the monks were gathering stones too, and Petroc took two corners of Margiad's sling from her so that it hung between them, carrying his own in his right hand.

'Too rough to stay down here any longer,' he said. 'Come on you two. Up the path as quick as you can.'

Heads down, the bedraggled group climbed up the path, carrying their heavy loads. Willing hands helped them from the top and the onshore gale blew them towards the new huts being built a little way down the path towards the village. They all emptied their stones in a heap and left the slings inside the wall of the hut that was almost complete.

But someone was calling again. Gylan turned and saw his father and Idwal standing buffeted by the gale at the top of the cliffs, their hands shading their eyes as they looked out to sea. He turned and ran back into the gale to the cliff top.

'What is it? Is it the raiders?' he cried and stood next to Gyffes peering out into the heaving mass of muscled grey and the pouring rain.

'No. "T"is Morgan and Cadoc. They went out on the tide when they thought the storm was over, but it's got worse and they're trying come ashore here. Can't get up the river with the tide still running out,' shouted Gyffes, above the wind.

Appalled, Gylan forced his eyes to look through the lashing wet. Still some way offshore between the little island that rose out of the sea, and the storm lashed beach, he glimpsed the small boat, bucking like an angry horse on the swollen waves, and the two men in her paddling frantically for the shore.

'Won't the wind blow them in?' he shouted.

'The wind's whipping up a big sea,' said Petroc, joining them, his heavy monk's habit swirling round his legs. 'But the tide'll take them out. They'll be exhausted in a few minutes.'

'What can we do?' wailed Gylan. 'We can't just leave them.'

'We need ropes,' said Gyffes, 'and a boat.'

'And everyone to pull,' said Idwal. 'We've a boat up here. Come on brothers. Let's get it down to the shore.'

'What will you do?' asked Margiad shivering with cold and huddling next to Gylan.

## Storm

'Weight some ropes with wood,' said Gyffes. 'Tie another rope to our boat and hang on to it. Let the tide take it out once we've launched it and throw the rope with the wood to Morgan and Cadoc – if we can. We'll need everyone back on shore to hang on to the shore rope. Down you go again. Don't fall. You're no use if you're wounded.'

Down on the beach they could no longer see Morgan and Cadoc or even the island. The waves were too high, and the spray and the rain stung their eyes.

'Merciful God,' muttered Gylan, through gritted teeth. 'Help us now. Please help us now.' He could feel Margiad clinging to his sodden cloak and he grasped her other hand.

'We'll do it,' he shouted to her. 'We'll get them in.' But he wasn't sure.

The monks were bringing their little boat down the cliff path step by step, heads down against the gale and watching each footfall. At last they reached the shore and were hurrying to the sea, while Gyffes, Idwal and Petroc tied wooden spars to the ends of ropes and wound the ropes into loops. Gylan and Margiad followed them all to the shoreline and stood with their backs to the water, watching the preparations. Idwal stowed two ropes weighted with the spars into the boat while Gyffes secured a third rope to the stern of the boat. A wave sizzled round their legs.

# Idwal's Bell

The monks pushed the boat further into the water and Gyffes shouted to Idwal and Margiad, 'Hang on to the end of the stern rope while we launch. Take it right back as far as you can without pulling the boat, so we have plenty of room to grab it once the boat is afloat.'

Shaking they did as they were told, and the monks and Gyffes waded into the shallow waves, pushing the boat.

'Right! Now HEAVE!' roared Gyffes and all together, shoulders straining and heads down they bore into the water. The boat reared up against the waves and smacked down again and the men staggered backwards.

'Once again!' bellowed Gyffes. 'HEAVE!' and once again the prow pointed to the dark purple sky and then plunged back into the water.

'Stay where you are,' shouted Gyffes as the wave washed through them, chest high.

'Now once again' – HEAVE!'

This time the boat moved forward, and Petroc and Idwal lunged over its sides on their bellies while the other men kept pushing. Margiad and Gylan moved a few steps down the beach, gripping the rope with icy hands, and saw Idwal and Petroc grasp the paddles and start trying to propel the boat seawards.

## Storm

As the wave swept back the boat plunged forwards, and Gylan and Margiad found themselves flat on the wet sand, still grasping the rope with numbing fingers.

'Well done,' called Gyffes, coming to help them. 'Get up! Keep hanging on. We're here now.'

He pulled them both to their feet, and the remaining eight monks grasped the rope, moving slowly towards the sea as Idwal and Petroc paddled out. Each receding wave sucked the boat out further now, and Gylan thought, 'How will we pull in two boats against the tide?'

Very soon the huge walls of foaming water hid the little boat, and Gyffes came back to Margiad.

'Go up to the top of the cliff,' he told her. 'Watch the boats. Idwal and Petroc will throw their ropes to Morgan and Cadoc. As soon and Morgan and Cadoc have got a rope in their boat wave with both arms above your head, so we know.'

Margiad nodded, and Gylan turned to watch her blown up the beach like a bedraggled chicken, and then slither and slip her way up the cliff path.

'Keep a hold on that rope,' shouted Gyffes, 'but don't pull it tight. We must let them get as close as they can,' and the foremost monks waded deep into the water as Idwal and Petroc progressed further out to sea.

## Idwal's Bell

Soon Gylan shivered chest deep in the foaming breakers, his feet struggling to find a grip in the stirring sand. His fingers were hooked round the rope, frozen into position, and he thought, 'It's nearly summer. This would kill us in the winter. It might kill Morgan and Cadoc now.'

The monks stepped further into the waves and Gylan gulped a mouthful of saltwater and retched.

'That's as far as we can go,' shouted Gyffes, now at the front of the line and up to his shoulders in water. He twisted round to look at Margiad, a crouched figure up in the wind, her hair whipping behind her.

Gylan raised his chin, gasping for breath, but the salt laden spray made him cough. He ducked, but a breaker slapped into his face and he coughed and spluttered again. 'Dear God, Holy Mother, help if you will.'

Then he remembered Idwal's words. 'I believe God helps those who help themselves,' and he dug his heels into the sand and tried to tighten his numbed fingers, raising his face defiantly against the churning water.

There was a shout. 'They have it! Right! All together on the shout! HEAVE!'

# Storm

Gylan never saw Margiad waving with both arms, high on the cliff above the waterfall, which thundered and splattered against the rocky face in the wind. He closed his eyes and pulled with the rest of them. The first pull was useless, and he found himself hauled back into the water, plunging his head under as he struggled to keep his feet on the sand and stand up, but Gyffes shouted again, and this time he could take a step backwards, praying that Morgan or Cadoc was paddling shorewards while the other clung to the wooden spar on the end of the rope. What were Idwal and Petroc doing? He supposed they would be paddling too but re-alised the rope would keep the stern of their boat facing the wrong way.

'Holy Mother, pray for us now,' he muttered. 'Holy Mother, pray for us.'

He dug his heels into the sand again and leant backwards. He stepped another step backwards, then slid forwards again. The monks heaved. They were trying to build up a rhythm, now but the tide was running out fast.

'If we could just stand still, if the wind would drop, we would make it,' thought Gylan despairing.

# Idwal's Bell

Then two white hands joined his on the end of the rope, and Margiad was beside him again, her long hair swirling in the water, and she flinging her small weight backwards with the next 'HEAVE!' and they took another step towards the shore.

Slowly, slowly, they inched out of the water, first Margiad and Gylan, then Conan, and then Trewis, till Petroc and Idwal's boat appeared on the crest of a wave, and as the wave crashed past it, Gyffes waded forward to seize it, and then all the monks were hauling it ashore, and then wading in to grab the second rope that pulled Morgan and Cadoc's tiny craft.

Gylan and Margiad sat on the sand, shivering and panting heavily. Gyffes came and put an arm round both of them.

'Well done,' he said, giving them an affectionate shake. Margiad glanced at Gylan and grinned, and he grinned back.

# Storm

For a few minutes everyone sat on the sand, with heads bowed against the wind and the spray, trying to catch their breath. They knew they had to get the boats up the cliff path or the next high tide would batter them against the rocks, so they struggled to their feet in their sodden clothes, shared themselves into two groups and lifted the boats, taking care not to spill the precious fish that lay in Morgan and Cadoc's and slowly progressed up the path. They stowed both the boats in the shelter of the new huts and sat down again to recover. Up on the cliff, the wind began to blow them dry.

'Thanks to all of you,' Morgan gasped eventually. 'Thank the good God you saw us.'

Cadoc nodded. 'I never did think all these defences were worth it,' he growled. 'A waste of time and effort, but I'm grateful you were up here today. We wouldn't have made it otherwise.'

Morgan shook his head. 'No,' he said. 'Thought the storm was dying down, but it wasn't. Always good pickings after a storm. We'll share out the fish'

'We were building the empty homes,' said Gylan, and Morgan and Cadoc looked at him.

'I know,' said Cadoc, 'and like I said, I don't think those raiders will come again. But without you all I wouldn't be sitting here now.'

Gylan saw Idwal smile to himself. He looked closely at Idwal's habit, seeing a red smear on his chest above the wetness of the wool, and when Idwal got up and walked back through the storm to the top of the waterfall, he and Margiad followed him.

'Idwal!' he called as they came up with him. 'Idwal! You're bleeding!'

Idwal stopped and turned to wait for them.

''T'is nothing,' he said.

But Gylan grasped the neck of Idwal's habit and pulled it down. Pinned to the inside was a silver woven brooch with five gemstones gleaming. He stared at Idwal in astonishment.

'What…?'

'Morwenna's.'

'Then why don't you wear it on the outside?' asked Gylan.

'It's beautiful,' said Margiad.

The rain started to wash away the blood where the brooch had scratched Idwal's chest.

'Monks don't wear fine baubles,' he said, with a wry smile. 'You know I killed a man. It's wrong to kill. I wear this so that it pierces my flesh sometimes, to remind me of what I did.'

'But he killed Morwenna!' protested Gylan.

'That doesn't make killing right.'

126

'It might make them afraid to come again,' said Gylan.

'Morgan and Cadoc don't think they'll come again,' said Margiad.

Idwal put a hand on the shoulder of each. 'He was their chief,' he said, his blue eyes solemn. 'He probably had sons. They will come again.'

## Chapter Eleven
### Listening

'Greg! Hurry up! They're crossing the grass!' Andy hissed down the chimney.

'Stinking Sturgeon! I'll never make it,' Greg muttered. 'Okay! I'll hide. Hey! Pull up the rope!'

Andy hoisted up the rope and he and Megan flattened themselves on the corrugated iron roof, hoping it was strong enough to hold them. The hot metal burned their legs and they shifted uncomfortably until their own shadows cooled the metal. They could hear Greg puffing and scraping and then a clunk. Scuffling sounds floated up the chimney, and then there was silence.

# Idwal's Bell

Outside, the chattering voices came closer, and a deeper voice shouted instructions. Megan pressed herself flatter still, silently cursing that she was wearing a bright yellow t-shirt and hoping the ridge of the kitchen wall would keep her and Andy out of sight. A key rattled in the kitchen door and the hinges creaked. Megan held her breath, praying that Greg was hidden.

'Hand me your saddles, take a carton of drink and offer your ponies a drink in the stream,' she heard the helper say, and she heard leather creaking, buckles chinking, a rustling as people took their lunches from their saddlebags, and a buzz of conversation. Then came a repeated light thudding as each saddle was placed on something, and light hoof beats as the corresponding ponies were led away to drink at the stream.

'I'll give them a quick wipe,' the helper said, and then the last pony had gone and the door was shut. Megan heard the key grate in the lock.

'He really does lock the door,' thought Megan, raising her head a fraction to glance at Andy. He was looking at her with raised eyebrows. She eased closer to the chimney to listen.

They heard businesslike footsteps approaching the fireplace.

# Listening

Megan held her breath again. Had Greg found somewhere safe? Something was dumped on the floor and she heard a scraping, clanking sound. The man was opening the oven door! Andy frowned and Megan shrugged. They would have to wait for Greg to tell them what was happening. She imagined him crouched in some dark corner, afraid even to breathe. She could hear rustling and muttering and the occasional curse. The guide was busy.

A gull cried from above and a breeze buffeted across the top of the chimney. Megan felt the wind whipping her curls and she tried to still them with her flat hand.

'Okay?' Andy mouthed.

She nodded. 'What about Greg?'

He shrugged again. 'He must be hidden somewhere.'

The sun blazed down. The stones reflected the heat and the corrugated iron roof grew hotter and Megan envied the riders eating their lunches in the shade of the oak trees, while the ponies nibbled the short grass. The rustlings and mutterings continued, though it was difficult to hear above the sea breeze. Half an hour passed and the man hadn't stopped to eat lunch.

## Idwal's Bell

Megan peered over the chimney edge as the door was unlocked and sunlight spilled into the kitchen. The helper picked up his lunch and went out into the refectory to eat it.

Fifteen minutes crawled by. Perspiration dripped off her forehead and fizzled dry on the tin roof. The trekkers returned, leading their ponies across the grass and into the refectory.

'Hullo there,' said the helper. 'All ready to go? Right. I'll bring out the saddles.'

It seemed to take an age to saddle up the ponies. Megan didn't think the man had cleaned the saddles, but no one seemed to notice. At last the kitchen door was shut, and the key turned in the lock, and Megan and Andy heard the hoof beats fading. They waited, and waited, until Andy raised his head and looked around.

He called down the chimney. 'Greg? You okay?'

'Yes,' Greg called back. 'I'm fine. Have they gone?'

'Yes! And there's no one around. You can come out now.'

He let the rope snake down the chimney shaft.

'Hang on!' called Greg. 'I've just thought of something.'

They could hear him opening the oven door and closing it again, and then he called, 'Okay.'

'D'you want us to pull you up?' asked Andy.

'You'll have to help,' said Greg. 'I've gone all wobbly.'

They felt his weight on the rope as he swung himself up and propped his feet against the chimney shaft. Andy and Megan pulled, and Greg half climbed until his friends reached in and hauled him out into the sunlight.

For a few moments, he sat shading his eyes and soaking up the warmth while Andy and Megan stared at him.

'You're filthy,' observed Megan. 'You'll have to wash your things before we go home.'

Greg pulled out the waist of his green t-shirt. 'Rats!' he uttered in dismay. Megan and Andy glanced at one another.

'You haven't seen the back,' Andy said. 'It's black with soot. And your trainers are covered in ash.'

Greg shrugged. 'If we have a swim, I'll wash my clothes and they can dry while we eat lunch. I'm really hungry. Let's just get down from here,' he said.

They looked around, but though they could hear voices from the beach, they could see no one. It was safe to climb down to the kitchen garden. They lowered the stake and climbed down the wall, relieved to stand in the shade.

'That's better,' breathed Greg. 'Thank God he didn't see me!'

'What happened?' asked Megan.

'Well, I couldn't see much,' began Greg. 'I hid in a little niche in the opposite side of the fireplace to the oven. They must have stored the cooking pots there or something. But I could hear, and it's definitely suspicious. And he does lock himself in.'

Megan and Andy nodded. 'We heard the key go,' said Andy.

'Well, he said he was going to wipe the saddles over,' continued Greg, 'but he didn't. There's a couple of thick poles fixed on legs, and he puts the saddles on those. When the door's locked, he takes a tray of drinks, all sealed in plastic, from the oven over to the saddles. He had his back to me then, so I saw him do that. But he could have seen me if he'd turned round, so I hid again.'

'Drinks from the oven?' echoed Andy surprised, looping the rope.

'Yes. Not the ones from the pile in the fireplace. The riders have those for their lunch.'

'So what does he do?'

'I couldn't see. I heard him tear the plastic and I got the idea he was putting the cartons in the saddlebags.' Greg sat down on a large stone and ran his fingers through his hair.

## Listening

'Spare drinks for later?' suggested Megan.

'I thought that,' agreed Greg, 'but he brought the cardboard tray and the polythene and cartons back and put them in the oven again, only the cartons are empty!'

'How d'you know they're empty?' asked Andy, and Greg pulled a carton from his pocket.

'Look,' he said. 'He's ripped the bottom of the carton open. But the drink hasn't been drunk. The straw is still stuck on the side, and the little hole isn't pierced. But the carton is empty!'

Andy and Megan examined the carton carefully.

'It's dry inside,' observed Megan.

'So he put something from the cartons into the saddlebags?'

'And the riders didn't notice!'

'I don't know. Did you hear anything?'

Megan and Andy shook their heads. 'Nothing that sounded as if anyone was surprised,' said Andy.

'Maybe they never looked in their saddle bags,' said Greg.

'They must have done,' protested Megan. 'They must have put the rubbish from their lunches back in the saddlebags!'

# Idwal's Bell

Greg shrugged. 'Let's have a swim,' he said. 'I'll wash my clothes and we can have lunch. We'll think about it then.'

They dragged the stake back to the oak trees and collected their bags before crossing the grass to the cliff path.

Megan spun round, scanning the top of the cliff.

'What's the matter?' asked Andy.

'I heard some people running across the grass,' she said, looking behind her.

'Where?' Andy asked, looking too.

'Towards the path down to the village,' said Megan, still searching.

'I can't see anyone,' said Andy, 'And it's a track, not a path.'

'You've got the jumps because of Witherguts,' said Greg, stopping.

To their right the waterfall splashed down to its rainbowed pool before spilling out to the waves. Seagulls hung on taut wings over the cliffs and two families with small children were playing cricket on the beach.

'I expect you heard those children's footsteps,' said Greg. 'Not many people find this beach 'cos there's no car park.'

## Listening

But Megan kept looking round, convinced she'd heard footsteps running fast behind them.

'I s'pose there'll have to be a car park if the monastery becomes a tourist place,' said Andy, but Greg shook his head.

'It won't be near the monastery,' he said. 'Mum says Tom thinks it's important for people to walk up.'

'Why?' asked Andy.

Greg shrugged. 'I'm not sure. Something to do with the legend and the messenger I s'pose.'

Megan shivered and glanced behind again, feeling her heart beat faster.

'Oh. What did Tom say his name was?' asked Andy. 'Gil…Gil something?'

'Gylan,' said Megan with certainty. She looked across to the monastery and the waterfall, to the bell tower standing alone on her left, and beyond it to the beginning of the track that led down to the village, and he was there, sprinting terrified down the path… a fair haired boy in a tunic… someone with him…

Panic poured through her and she fought to control an impulse to run for her life.

'That's right. Gylan,' said Greg. 'You've got a good memory, Megs.'

From ages past. She was as frightened as Gylan had been when they ran and ran, and ran…

'I wonder what Alan Wetherton is up to,' said Andy.

Megan looked out to the empty horizon and the panic subsided. Someone on the beach was flying a kite and it dipped and swooped in the sky above the cliffs. She forced Gylan from her mind and trotted down the cliff path after Andy and Greg, who washed his t-shirt, shorts, and trainers in the pool beneath the waterfall. This was not entirely successful, but they looked better, and he spread them out on a rock to dry.

They dived and splashed in the glittering waves for half an hour and then decided they needed lunch and raced up the beach to their bags.

'Hmmmmm, that's good,' said Andy, biting into a ham sandwich. 'It must be late.'

Greg rummaged in his bag for his phone. 'It's two thirty!' he exclaimed. 'Late for lunch anyway. Especially after all that excitement.'

'So do we tell someone what we saw?' said Andy.

'Who?' asked Megan, biting into a cold sausage.

'Our parents, or the Police,' said Andy. 'We think he's doing something he shouldn't, so we ought to tell the police.'

'But what do we say?' protested Greg, stuffing his phone back in his bag. 'I didn't see the helper do anything wrong. And I shouldn't have been there!'

'So why does he lock the door, and say he's going to clean the saddles when he doesn't?' Andy pointed out, waving his ham sandwich about and attracting a group of gulls.

'He'll say it's for security,' said Megan.

'What we need,' said Andy, throwing away a crust and selecting an energy bar from his lunchbox, 'is proof. A full carton from the oven.'

'You mean it's not drink in the carton?' queried Greg.

'Can't be if the empty carton is as dry as the one you brought out. But if he rips the bottom open, something must've been taken out.'

Greg snapped his fingers. 'I wish I'd thought of bringing a full one.'

'You didn't know they were dry at the time,' Megan pointed out kindly, waving her arms to shoo away an interested Herring gull. 'Go away! This is my lunch. Not yours!'

'True,' said Greg, throwing his crusts to the gull and attracting several more. 'And they'd probably know straightaway if one was missing.'

Andy frowned. 'I wonder which cartons he brought last night,' he said. 'He must have brought the real drink cartons up in his Range Rover on Sunday when Auntie Liz saw him. Enough to last the week.'

'If that's right, the ones he brought ashore last night are the ones he hid in the oven,' added Greg.

'So he doesn't want anyone to see those,' Megan said, hurling crusts as far as she could.

'No! He brings them when it's dark,' agreed Greg. 'He hides them, and the helper locks the kitchen door while he puts whatever is in them into the saddlebags.'

'And he doesn't want the monastery to become a tourist site!' added Megan.

'Because then he can't hide stuff in the kitchen,' finished Andy.

They stared at each other in triumph. Megan put her head in her hands.

'What's the matter Megs?' Asked Greg.

'I just keep having this feeling someone's trying to tell us something.'

'Feelings now!' exclaimed Andy. 'For God's sake! First it was the bell. Then it was footsteps. Now it's feelings! Go away, will you!'

He stood up and shooed away the gulls.

# Listening

'I can't help it,' protested Megan, her green eyes bright. 'I'm not making it up, and it's not much fun!'

'It's that fortune teller,' said Greg. 'What else did she say?'

'She said someone was anxious,' said Megan, shrugging and trying to look unconcerned.

'Well, we have been,' said Greg. 'I was scared when Witherguts turned up this morning.'

'You can make it mean anything you want,' said Andy. 'You could make up any old rubbish to make it fit.'

'Think, Megs,' urged Greg again.

'She said something round and old and sharp was important,' said Megan.

'I thought the shadow was old,' said Andy. 'See? It's all muddled now. I bet it wasn't like you say at all. You're just talking drivel.'

Megan shook her head. 'The shadow was different,' she said. 'That was a person.'

'Okay. What sort of person?' Andy asked, waving his arms at the seagulls as they gathered to approach again.

And suddenly Megan knew, but couldn't say it.

'What sort of person?' Andy persisted, sitting down.

'Someone with a scar,' Megan replied at last, while inside a voice said, 'Idwal.'

'Scar? How d'you know he had a scar?' demanded Andy.

'I thought I saw his face in the crystal ball,' muttered Megan. 'I expect I imagined it,' and then she thought, *Why did I say that? I didn't imagine it.*

'Course you did!' exclaimed Andy. 'Pathetic! Crystal ball? You never mentioned that before.'

'Because I knew you wouldn't believe me,' snapped Megan. 'And I was right, wasn't I? You don't, even though it was you who made me go!'

'Well it's just a load of stupid rubbish,' said Andy. 'I said so when you first told us about it.'

'It's fun though,' said Greg. 'It's really cool. Some of it fits. The monastery's old.'

'But not round and sharp,' retorted Andy. 'We've got enough to think about without shadows and old sharp things.'

'So what do we do?' asked Greg.

'We need one of those cartons,' insisted Andy.

'I told you,' said Greg. 'They'd know someone had found them. They're wrapped up in plastic on their cardboard tray, like you see them arrive in the shops. I'd have to break open the plastic to get one off the tray.'

'But they won't know who,' pointed out Andy.

'And if we go straight to the police,' said Megan, rallying her concentration, 'they won't find out in time. The police will find Alan Wetherton before he finds the opened pack.'

142

Greg grinned. 'Down the chimney again!' he said. 'Still, it should be easier a second time.'

'I'll go this time,' said Andy. 'You've had your turn.'

'Or I could go,' put in Megan.

'Oh yeah,' mocked Andy. 'You're frightened of shadows, and footsteps that aren't there. Can't see you going down the chimney!'

'Come on,' said Greg, standing up. 'We can argue on the way to fetch the stake.'

They stuffed the remains of their lunches into their bags and Greg felt his clothes to see if they were dry. They were still damp but he said the sun and wind would soon finish the job, and he pulled them on and they hurried up the cliff path.

But when they reached the top, a family of sightseers was looking round the monastery, and Tom Merthen was there once again, this time with two men who were taking measurements.

'Well that's that then,' said Greg. 'We can't go down the chimney while anyone else is here!'

'During the building of this footbridge, ancient wooden piles were found on the north side and in the bed of the river.

After a detailed archaeological survey it has been concluded that the bridge is built on the site of the fortifications erected to defend the village against the Vikings after the raid in AD 981.

# Chapter Twelve
# On Their Way

There were no guest cars in the drive and all seemed quiet when they arrived at the house, until they went through the kitchen doorway. There they were greeted by Mum who cried at once, 'Oh great! I was just coming to find you. The twins are on their way and I'm taking Liz and Rob to the maternity unit in Tremarron. I'll come back as soon as I can. There are guests staying tonight, but they won't be back till late, and I'm going to put the 'Full' sign up to stop any more coming tonight, and I've told the Tourist Information Centre too, so there shouldn't be any problems.' She stopped to draw breath. 'I won't be very long. Can you get yourselves some tea later? I don't like leaving you.'

144

'That's all right Mrs Williams,' said Greg, his big eyes reassuring her through his spectacles. 'They can come down to mine for tea. I'll phone my mum.'

'Oh Greg, are you sure?'

'Of course,' said Greg. 'Mum won't mind.'

He rummaged in his bag and triumphantly drew out his phone. 'I'll call her now. She'll still be at work, but that's okay.'

'And Mum,' said Megan, suddenly inspired, 'If we go to Greg's for tea, could he come back here to spend the night?'

'Well yes' said Mum, searching her handbag for her car keys. 'So long as it's all right with his mother. I expect she knows Liz, does she Greg?'

'Ever so well,' said Greg, his phone to his ear, 'because of Gran doing the ironing.'

'Oh yes' said Mum, relieved. 'They must be in here somewhere. Where have I put them? So I'll expect you back this evening. Greg, would you leave your phone number and your address, just in case?'

''Course I will,' soothed Greg. 'I'll write them down and leave them in the kitchen for you to see when you come back.'

Mum hurried out the kitchen, calling over her shoulder, 'Perhaps you three could put Auntie Liz's case in the car for me? It's at the foot of the stairs.'

# Idwal's Bell

'Not if you've lost the car keys,' muttered Andy.

Greg found a notepad and pencil and wrote his home details, while Andy picked up the suitcase, and Megan found the car keys in the kitchen drawer. Uncle Rob hopped across the hall on his crutches.

'Good thing you came home,' he said. 'We were going to phone Greg but we haven't got his number! Take care, won't you? Don't do anything silly. What a time to break a leg!'

Megan smiled at him and turned to Greg in time to see a look of innocent surprise. She went out to open the car, and Uncle Rob hopped after her as Mum and Auntie Liz came out the front door. Auntie Liz was walking gingerly, Megan thought.

'Good luck Auntie Liz,' she said. 'We'll see you soon!'

Auntie Liz nodded to her and sat carefully in the back of the car while Andy stowed the suitcase in the boot. He shut the lid.

'There you go,' he said.

Mum slid into the driver's seat, switched on the engine and Megan and Andy retreated to the doorway where they were joined by Greg.

'Do take care!' called Mum. 'I'll see you later!' She hauled on the steering wheel and gravel squirted as the car turned and accelerated towards the gate.

'How long does it take to reach Tremarron?' asked Megan.

'At least forty minutes,' said Greg gleefully. 'Depends on the traffic. She won't be back for quite a while.'

'Did you put your phone number on the pad in the kitchen?' asked Megan.

'No,' said Greg. 'Just my address and the landline number. The signal's dodgy here anyway.'

'Or is it just that you don't want people calling you?' asked Megan.

Greg looked defiant. 'My Mum knows my number,' he said. 'But what's the point if I'm not with my phone?'

'You carry it in your pocket, you idiot,' said Andy. 'If I had a phone I'd keep it with me.'

'Yeah, but we don't want them to know we're going down the chimney, do we? My mum doesn't call me so long as she thinks she knows where I'm going. And I can call her if I need to. Anyway, we've got to decide what to do next.'

'Tom hasn't come down from the monastery,' observed Andy. 'He could be up there ages.'

'Lots of village people go up there in the evenings,' said Greg. 'It's a favourite walk.'

'So it'll be difficult to get down the chimney,' said Megan, turning to go back into the house. 'We'd better go down to Greg's and think while we eat tea.'

**147**

## Idwal's Bell

Greg lived in a cottage behind the shops on the harbour. The ground sloped, you could see the roofs of the houses below from the kitchen window. His mother was small, pretty and smiling and didn't seem surprised at the state of his t-shirt, saying she would soak it in some stain remover and please would he not do the same thing, whatever it was, to the t-shirt he was going to put on instead.

'Our Mum would go ballistic if we got our t-shirts that dirty,' said Andy, but Greg shrugged and said his mother was used to it.

'Sometimes I climb the cliffs to get Samphire,' he added. 'I always come home mucky then.'

'Isn't it dangerous to climb the cliffs?' said Megan, but Greg shrugged again.

'Depends where you climb,' he said. 'Some bits are not so steep; then it's easy.'

His father was still out to sea, fishing, and wouldn't be home until much later, so his mother suggested they eat a picnic tea in the tiny, sloping garden at the back of the cottage. She loaded them with sandwiches, crisps, fruit and chocolate biscuits, and they sat at the top of the garden and ate in near silence, each one thinking hard.

Suddenly Greg sat up straight and said, 'Where does he get the other drinks from?'

'We don't know,' said Andy, puzzled. 'He brought them off a rowing boat.'

'Exactly. So they were on his posh boat before that.'

'They must've been,' said Andy frowning.

'So why don't we go and look on his boat?'

'We can't do that,' said Megan, round eyed.

'Why not?' said Greg.

'We don't know what it looks like,' said Andy, 'or where it is.'

'I do,' said Greg grinning. 'I told you. He goes fishing round Gull Island. I've seen him go, and his boat's called Hot Stuff.'

'Wow! What a name!' Exclaimed Andy.

'Where does he keep it?' Asked Megan, pulling up grass and piling it into a little heap.

'I'm not sure,' said Greg. He frowned. 'There are a couple of mooring places in the harbour. I've never seen his boat in the one by the pier that divides the harbour from the river. It's probably further over near the lifeboat house.'

'Where's that?' asked Andy. 'I didn't know there was one.'

'On the other side of the river, past the first moorings. There's a metal runway out to the lifeboat house so the men can run along it to the lifeboat.'

'Why?' asked Megan, trying to visualise this urgent dash.

## Idwal's Bell

'The lifeboat's launched down a slipway straight into deep water,' Greg explained. 'The runway's so the men run from the shore to the lifeboat to save time.'

'Oh,' said Megan, still doubtful.

'But not for much longer,' said Greg. ''Cos we're getting a new lifeboat soon. Keep us up to date. It's a busy lifeboat. We can go and have a look when I've collected my stuff. It's in the opposite direction from here, but that doesn't matter. We can go back to yours afterwards.'

'Does Alan Wetherton often fish at night?' asked Andy, licking his chocolaty fingers.

'I dunno.' Greg shrugged. 'He can't fish in the day if he's trekking all the time. Have you two finished? We want time to find this boat. I'll get my stuff. I won't need much. Just pyjamas and a sleeping bag.'

When he had gathered these, and a change of clothes, they thanked his mother for tea and told her they were going across the river before returning to Auntie Liz's house and walked down the steep path that led to the road between the shops and the river, Greg carrying his gear in his big bag.

It was early evening, but the July sun was still high and the air was warm. At the end of the road was a small car park, almost full.

## On Their Way

The shops were open, making the most of the summer trade, and opposite them the River Ros argued fruitlessly with the sea, making angry chattering noises as current opposed current. Greg led Andy and Megan towards the river and then swung inland towards a footbridge.

'The road bridge you came over when you came is further up the river,' he told them. 'Look! You can see the lifeboat station.' He pointed across the river to where a large white boxlike structure stood some distance away on strong metal stilts above the deepening waves.

'See? It's out to sea even at low tide, so the lifeboat runs down the ramp into deep water. You should see her go! She makes an amazing splash!'

'Have you seen it then?' asked Andy enviously

'Loads of times. If I hear the maroon I run out to watch. Sometimes, when the weather is really rough, and it's pouring with rain, you can't see the lifeboat station. You just hear the klaxon that warns you she's going. Come on. We've got to cross the bridge.'

'Hang on,' said Megan. 'What's this?' she pointed to a plaque on the metal pillar of the footbridge.

'Oh that's about the old fortifications. It's quite interesting.'

### Idwal's Bell

Megan read aloud,

ST IDWAL'S FOOTBRIDGE
RIVER ROS

'During the building of this footbridge, ancient wooden piles were found on the north side and in the bed of the river. After a detailed archaeological survey it has been concluded that the bridge is built on the site of the fortifications erected to defend the village against the Vikings after the raid in AD 981 …'

'Come on Megs! We've got to find this boat!' said Andy tugging her t-shirt.

'I haven't finished. It says more,' protested Megan hanging back.

'Read it another day! We've got to look at this boat before Mum starts to get worried.' He ran on to the bridge.

But Megan stood rooted, gripping the railings at the side of the riverbank, staring at the bridge. There were five arches, two small ones at each side and a much larger central one to let the bigger vessels through. The Ros swirled around the iron piers, muttering and gurgling, and soon the sea would retreat, and the river pour more and more freely, swiftly and eagerly purposeful out to sea.

'Don't fall in!' A passing teenaged boy thumped her between the shoulder blades and she lurched forward, quickly regaining her balance, yet imagining with horrible reality plummeting into that cold, strong water, fighting to reach air, struggling to grab the piers as the river hauled her away. She was tense with cold, her gasping lungs compressed with the current, the bank almost unreachable…

'Megan! Come on!'

She started at Andy's angry call but glanced back into the river where a wild – eyed, terrified white face under wet flaxen hair focussed fixedly up at her.

'Come on!' she shouted, and the boy struck out for the river bank that had no railings, just mud and a strange bucket…

# Idwal's Bell

'Megan!'

And all was gone.

'Okay, okay, but it may be important.'

Halfway across the footbridge she stopped and looked behind. Beyond the houses of the village she could see the track to the cliff top, leading past Auntie Liz's house, and disappearing into the fold of the rise. Just above that the bell tower pointed into the clear sky.

'Look!' called Megan.

'What now?' Andy and Greg waited on the other side of the river.

'You can see the cliff path going up to the monastery.'

'Track, you mean. So what?'

'If this was where the fortifications were, they could see if anyone was coming down the cliff,' Megan persisted.

'Or up the river. 'Course they could, Ninny! Why d'you think they put them there?'

'And they would hear the bell.'

'If it rang,' said Andy. 'That's the idea of bells. Come on, Megs!'

'Okay, okay. But it may be important.' Megan looked back.

'How can 981 be important now?' said Andy. 'They didn't have drink cartons then!'

## On Their Way

Greg giggled, but an unease gripped Megan's chest. 'I wanted to finish reading that,' she argued but Andy was hurrying on and she turned to join him, thinking 'Fortifications! To defend themselves if the Vikings came back. And there's the bell tower up on the cliff. So they could warn everyone. They must've been terrified.' Her eyes widened and her fists clenched as she imagined the horror, imagined the Vikings pouring down the cliff path…

By now the tide was full, and the boats moored along the harbour wall floated high, rising and curtseying with the swelling waves. Megan followed Andy and Greg, walking along towards the lifeboat house, reading the boat names as they went.

'*Windlassie, Peggoty, Zephyr, Madeleine,*' counted Andy as they passed.

'*Storm Petrel, Western Opal, Nigella, Isoswift*, that's a good one,' said Greg.

'*Marianina, Quest, Morgan Le Fey*, there are loads. Where is it?'

Greg hurried on down the line. When he had reached the last boat before the lifeboat runway, he turned and waved. 'Here she is,' he cried. 'Hot Stuff!'

Andy and Megan ran to join him and stood staring at the boat in front of them, a smart red motor launch with a sizeable rowing boat tied astern.

'It's big,' said Megan.

'Huge,' agreed Andy. 'It's got a cabin and a back bit and everything.'

'He would need the rowing boat to get ashore,' said Greg. He stepped down on to the narrow pontoon that ran alongside Hot Stuff and went to look at the tender. Then he turned and beckoned. Megan and Andy followed.

'Look. There are no oars nor outboard.

Just a pile of waterproof sheeting. I expect they're locked in the cabin.'

'Then how do we look in the boat if it's locked?' asked Megan.

'We can't,' said Greg.

# Chapter Thirteen
## The Hay Harvest
### AD 994

Gylan's back ached. All day he had carried hay to be stored for the winter and now he lay on a sweet smelling pile of it, staring up at the clear spring sky. The crop was heavy. Spring had come late, but it had come mild and damp and everything was growing apace and was plentiful. The sun was still high and warm on his tired limbs. He lay drowsing, glad to be resting for a few moments.

'Gylan! Gylan!'

He knew the voice at once for Margiad was rarely far from him. He sat up.

'Gylan! Where are you?'

'I'm here! I was having a rest.'

# Idwal's Bell

Her red hair had come loose from its crown and nape fastenings and floated around her. Her green eyes sparkled in anticipation as she ran up to him.

'Come on! They're starting the feast. You should put on your cloak.'

'It's too hot for a cloak. What does it matter what we wear?'

Margiad made an impatient sound. 'Well hurry anyway or you'll miss the start.'

Gylan rolled over and stood up. 'If I put on my cloak, you have to do your hair,' he bargained.

'All right. Meet you there,' and she was gone, running and leaping like a roe deer, her hair streaming behind her.

Gylan jogged home to fetch his blue cloak with its silver clip. His new tunic was blue, dyed with the woad that grew by the hut, the colour fixed with salt from the sea. His mother bought the woad seeds from a pedlar years ago, and all the family's best clothes were blue, except for Gyffes's dark red cloak made from cloth bought from the same pedlar. Everyone wore their best clothes to a feast, and Gylan grinned at the thought of appearing in a bright colour, and perhaps being allowed to drink some mead. He knew Margiad's mother had made her a plaid dress, but she had nothing blue.

## The Hay Harvest

*Nor has Branoc*, thought Gylan with satisfaction.

His mother had baked two batches of scones on the griddle above the fire, and next to the flames a tray of corncakes sat on a hot stone, turning to an appetising gold. Flagons of mead stood by the door, their heady, honey fragrance cloying the air. Rhianna wore a bronze circlet on her arm, and she chattered incessantly. Gyffes darkened the doorway, big and fair in his finest clothes with a jewelled clasp fastening his crimson cloak.

'Ready?' he asked, smiling at them like a happy giant. 'Let's go!'

Laden with food they followed him from the house to the long tables set up before the barn where already many of the villagers were chattering and laughing, glad to have the hay in and a fine evening to celebrate. Gylan breathed deeply, savouring the spicy woodsmoke from the glowing fire, the richness of slowly roasting meat, the heavy sweetness of mead and elderberry wine, and the warm crispness of freshly baked bread. In one corner a group of children were playing a circle game, and in another the musicians were warming up. Drumbeats pattered, pipe notes rippled, and Bren's lilting voice lifted on the mild evening air.

# Idwal's Bell

Brythen the smith raised two flagons high. The villagers hushed. He gave thanks for the abundance of the hay harvest and said, 'Let's celebrate! Hold out your cups, friends,' and he went among the villagers, offering each one mead or elderberry wine, to drink to a good summer and a plentiful harvest to come.

So the feast began. A drinking horn lay by a flagon. Gylan glanced around and grabbed it, half filled it with mead, and gulped furtively. Its syrupy tang tingled the back of his nose and throat. His teeth tore at flat bread, roasted meat and corncakes. He sang in the choruses, and despite Branoc and Conan's sniggers, danced with Margiad, who had tamed her hair and wore a necklace made from shells.

Everyone was there, the monks from the monastery, the fisher folk, farmers and craftsmen, wives, mothers and children. Except Idwal. Gylan searched the merrymaking, feasting crowd. Where was Idwal? Of course! If all the other monastery dwellers were here, then Idwal would be watching at the top of the waterfall. The music grew louder, the dancing faster. The flagons were passed round and round again. Everyone was laughing, weary, happy. Why should Idwal miss it all?

## The Hay Harvest

Gylan went to his father who was asking Bren to sing another song. He tugged at Gyffes's sleeve.

'Can I take a flagon to Idwal?'

Gyffes looked down at him. 'Idwal? Isn't he here?'

'He won't leave the waterfall without a look-out.'

'Then take him a flagon, and some corn cakes. It's a shame to miss the feast.' He glanced at the sun. 'It'll be light a while yet but be careful on the path. And don't forget your staff!'

'You always say that!' said Gylan.

'Shame on you that I have to,' said his father.

'There won't be any wolves up at the monastery,' said Gylan crossly.

'No. But can I trust you not to go off anywhere else?'

'I won't.' Gylan turned abruptly to go in search of a full flagon of mead.

'Blueyboy, Blueyboy, I dare you drink some mead!' cried Branoc, snatching at his sleeve while Conan danced in front of him, his sharp nose reddened with drinking wine.

'I've had some, Slugwit,' retorted Gylan, shrugging him off. 'Drunken fools. I'm going to find Idwal.'

'Why? Is he lost? Again? He lost his way years ago!' taunted Conan. 'Stay and try some wine. Here's your little friend. Give her some mead. Never mind that silly monk!'

'Go and jump in the river!' growled Gylan, picking up a full flagon. 'It might sober you up!'

'Gylan! What're you doing?' Margiad was at his side, her chest heaving from an energetic dance, and her hair sliding from its clips.

'Taking this to Idwal. He must be watching at the waterfall. Can you find some corn cakes for me to take?'

'Of course. I'll come with you.'

'No, Margiad. Stay and enjoy the dancing. I won't be long.'

But Margiad shook her head. 'You go on with the mead,' she said, 'and I'll follow when I've found some cakes.'

Gylan pushed through the noisy crowd and hurried past the deserted part of the village to the fortifications. He climbed a ladder and slid one down the far side so that he could get down. The fortifications were unmanned. Careful not to slop the mead, he trudged up the path towards the monastery. The music grew fainter and he could see the bell tower reaching upwards before him.

## The Hay Harvest

The sun was hanging in the western sky, flushing the white walls of the empty homes to soft pink as he passed them. He topped the rise, and there was Idwal sitting crosslegged looking out to sea, the sunlight on his face. Gylan stopped. A gull glided silently past him. A pair of red-legged choughs swooped and tumbled like aerial acrobats almost over Idwal's head, their black feathers gleaming as they caught the sun.

'He's so good,' thought Gylan. 'He watches out for us all the time and lots of the villagers laugh at him for it. It's thirteen years since they came, after all.'

As though Idwal could hear Gylan's thoughts, he turned and waved. The sun lit the scar on his strong face.

'But he'll never forget. Nor will Dad and Mahme. Nor will poor Eywy.' He waved back and hurried across the grass.

'I brought you some mead,' he cried. 'You're missing all the fun!'

'I can hear some of it,' said Idwal. 'The music is splendid.'

'And Bren's singing,' added Gylan, 'and Margiad is finding you some corn cakes. I told her to stay and enjoy the dancing, but she wanted to come.

'One of the best dancers in the village,' said Idwal, 'and a good girl all round. Pretty too! You could do worse, Gylan.'

'I know,' said Gylan blushing. 'But it's too soon yet. I knew you'd be here,' he said, sitting down. 'The hay's all in.'

'I thought it must be,' chuckled Idwal. 'Else why the feast? It was a good crop. The animals will be well fed in the winter.'

'We spend all spring and summer preparing for winter!' grumbled Gylan, and Idwal laughed.

'We make the most of what the earth gives us and try to look after it in return,' he said. 'We can't do without sun, earth and water.'

'Or God,' said Gylan.

'Or God,' agreed Idwal.

A shout made them turn towards the path, and there was Margiad, waving and smiling, with a cloth bundle in one hand.

'Honey cakes!' she said as she came closer. 'Here you are Idwal. These are the ones I made. I hope they're good.' She spread out the cloth on the grass before Idwal, revealing six little honey-colour-ed cakes. 'Try one,' she invited.

Idwal picked one up and bit into it, closing his eyes while he chewed.

'Delicious,' he declared. 'So you are a good cook too!' He raised his eyebrows at Gylan who blushed again.

Margiad laughed and sat down by the edge of the cliff and leaned over.

'Come back! You're too close!' said Idwal.

'I like to watch the water gushing down,' said Margiad, but she wriggled back, and they all looked down at the splashing waterfall, transformed into a fairy shower of rainbow droplets as the sun lowered.

Gylan reached for a honeycake, but Margiad pushed his hand away. 'They're Idwal's,' she said. 'You've eaten lots already.'

'How do you know?'

'I saw you. And you drank some mead.'

'You don't have to watch me all the time!' grumbled Gylan, but Idwal laughed.

'What's the good of a feast if you can't eat?' he said. 'It's too nice an evening to quarrel.'

'It's beautiful,' said Gylan looking out towards the island and watching two cormorants winging across the waves. 'The sea's so bright.'

Idwal looked up from his honey cake and out of habit swept the horizon with his eyes. Then he froze.

'Have some mead,' suggested Gylan, offering him the flagon, but Idwal didn't move.

'Idwal?'

No response, and Gylan turned to look after his gaze. To the right on the horizon he could make out tiny shapes against a pale gold sky.

'What is it? They're fishing boats aren't they? Going into Tremarron.'

Idwal stood up, staring out to the advancing shapes. Shapes not like fishing boats, but long and slender with uplifted prows and bright square sails bellied with the westerly breeze. Horrified, Gylan and now Margiad became aware of a rhythmic glint on the sides of each vessel, as the sun caught a regular, steady movement.

'Oars!' croaked Idwal, straining his eyes. 'Thirteen years and his sons are grown!' He turned to Gylan and Margiad. 'Run! Warn everyone! If I ring the bell now, they'll hear it and hurry. Tell the women and children to take the livestock up to the forest. Man the defences; boil the fat and water. I'll ring the bell when they're close and they'll come here and not up the river. Hurry! Now!'

Gylan and Margiad had scrambled to their feet, scattering the cakes and flagon, but Gylan clung to Idwal's habit, his eyes wide.

'They're feasting!' he cried. 'The mead's gone round loads of times. They won't heed us!'

'They must! Look how many there are! Five or six boats, loaded with men!'

Margiad, covered her face with her hands, 'Holy Mary, Holy Mother....'

'What shall I say? There's no one on watch!'

'Fools! Here! Take this!' Reaching inside his habit Idwal tore out the big, silver, woven brooch, set with gemstones. 'Take it to Gyffes. He'll know. Hurry!'

'What about you? You must hide when they come.'

'Go!' shouted Idwal terribly. 'NOW!'

'Come with us Idwal. I don't want you to be hurt.'

Idwal clasped the two of them close.

'Listen! I am with you! Part of me will always be watching. Now run! Go as fast as you can, and God go with you!'

He kissed the tops of their heads, pushed them away, and turned back to the reddening ocean, a bold figure silhouetted against the sunset sky, and Gylan and Margiad fled, their feet thudding across the cliff top and down the path to the village, with Morwenna's brooch clutched fast in Gylan's right hand.

## Chapter Fourteen
## Under Wraps

'Of course, anything suspicious would be locked away,' said Andy. 'We should have thought of that.'

'Well I'm going to have a look anyway,' said Greg. 'Keep a look out. I don't want to be caught like I was down the chimney!'

'We'll keep watch,' Megan reassured him, but Greg was already climbing on to the back of the Hot Stuff, his eyes gleaming, while Megan and Andy patrolled the sea wall. In less than three minutes he was back beside them.

'Nothing,' he said.

Andy was staring towards the river. Several people were walking up and down the sea wall, enjoying the summer evening, but one looked familiar.

'It's him!'

'Where?'

Andy nodded towards an approaching figure dressed in jeans, a black t-shirt and carrying a thick black sweater.

'There, look. Walking towards us by the *soswift*. If I point he'll notice.'

'Pretend to be looking at the lifeboat runway,' said Greg. 'We'll watch him without his knowing.'

They wandered past the Hot Stuff and sat on the sea wall staring at the lifeboat station. Footsteps approached.

Greg turned and beamed at him. 'Hullo Mr Wetherton.'

'Evening,' said Alan Wetherton, glancing at them disinterestedly. He jumped on to the Hot Stuff and she rocked in the water, sending waves slapping against the runway pillars.

Andy, Megan and Greg strained their ears to catch any sound but by glancing furtively sideways they saw him unlock the cabin door and go inside. He reappeared carrying the outboard motor and grasping the painter of the rowing boat, stepped aboard her and slotted the motor into position. Next, he fetched the oars and put them down in the stern of the Hot Stuff. He paused, searched the boat and exclaimed in annoyance. He jumped onto the little pontoon and hurried back towards the river.

'He's forgotten something,' exclaimed Andy.

'And he hasn't locked the cabin. Now's our chance!' said Greg.

While Alan Wetherton was still striding away, the three of them tore round to the pontoon and in seconds were on board the Hot Stuff.

'She's pretty swish,' said Andy.

'You said it. Look at these walnut lockers!'

'And leather seats!'

'Megs, keep a look out.'

'Why me?' muttered Megan, but she halted and turned to survey the sea wall, thinking, *Why do I always do as I'm told?*

Feverishly the boys searched behind cushions and under seats but found nothing.

'Let's have another look outside,' suggested Greg. 'There's got to be something. C'mon Megan.'

They left the cabin and looked under the seats in the stern.

'What about under the sheeting in the rowing boat?' wondered Andy.

'Okay,' said Greg, and one after the other they climbed into the rocking skiff and lifted the heaped, plastic waterproof.

'Nothing,' said Andy disappointedly.

'He's coming!' hissed Megan. 'I couldn't see him behind the other boats!'

# Idwal's Bell

'Quick! Under here!' Andy lifted the blue plastic wrap and they all scrambled underneath and lay curled up while the boat lurched in the water. Waves smacked the sea wall and seconds later they heard Alan Wetherton board the Hot Stuff. He strode to the stern of the launch and they thought he had seen them. Then something light landed in the stern of the launch and the footsteps went away into the cabin. Silent seconds crawled past, and to Megan's horror, the engine roared into life.

'What on earth do we do now?' breathed Greg.

The Hot Stuff dipped and rocked and bumped against the rowing boat, throwing the stow-aways against one another. Then, rolling to starboard she turned and gathered speed, jerking the rowing boat into her wake and towing her out of the harbour.

'Don't know,' came Andy's voice in the dark, as he rubbed one knee. 'Keep quiet!'

'Stop rustling the plastic then,' Megan told him.

'He's bound to find us,' put in Greg.

'We've got to get out somehow,' said Andy. 'If only we knew where we're going.'

'If he's fishing, we're off to Gull Island,' said Greg. 'Get off my foot, Andy!'

'All night?' gasped Megan. 'Mum will be worried sick!'

'No she won't,' said Andy, wriggling. 'I can't move any further! What about your phone, Greg?'

'It's in my bag,' said Greg, 'by the runway steps.'

'Oh great! You absolute idiot!' exploded Andy.

'I know,' groaned Greg. 'I'm really sorry. But I couldn't search the boat with that huge bag.'

'You friggin' halfwit! Why can't you keep your phone in your pocket?' Andy hissed, furious.

'It falls out,' said Greg. 'Gran told you, I've lost two. And if I put it in my back pocket, I sit on it.'

'Well put it on a string round your flippin' neck,' said Andy, bitterly. 'What use is it on the sea wall?'

'Shut up you two,' muttered Megan. 'Maybe someone will find it.'

'Yeah, and nick it,' said Andy. 'What's the time?'

'About eight thirty,' whispered Greg. 'When'll your Mum start worrying?'

'When it gets dark, I s'pose,' said Megan.

'Sun sets around 9.20,' said Greg. 'Last light just after 10 o'clock.'

'Don't be daft.' Andy lifted the edge of the plastic to look out, but Megan pulled it down again, hitting Greg a glancing blow as she did so.

'Ow!'

'Sh! It must get dark sooner than that.!'

'Well it doesn't,' retorted Greg, rubbing his nose. 'I check sunrise and sunset for Dad. And in June and July it's not properly dark all night.'

'Well our mum may phone your mum as soon as she's home to check everything's okay.'

'And my mum will tell her we've gone for a walk to look at the lifeboat before coming back. She won't worry then will she?'

'So no one will be looking for us,' groaned Megan. 'But there's nothing on the boat for Alan Wetherton to hide. Perhaps he won't be too angry.'

'We can't risk that,' said Andy. 'We haven't found the drink cartons, but that doesn't mean to say they're not here.'

'Maybe he's going to get them now,' said Greg. 'If we stop somewhere, say like Tremarron, we can get out.'

'Yeah and get a bus home,' said Andy.

'I haven't any money,' said Megan.

'Nor me,' said Andy.

Greg said nothing, not wanting to point out that he had money in his bag.

'So we're stuck,' muttered Andy. 'Great!'

For a while the only sound to be heard was the engine and the steady 'wash…wash…wash…' of the water. Megan imagined the sun sinking, glinting across the waves.

'How far is it to Tremarron?' she whispered.

'I couldn't tell you in sailing time,' Greg answered. 'It's a fair distance.'

Megan lapsed into silence. At least while Alan Wetherton was at the controls he couldn't look for them. She tried to work out ways of escape, but soon the boat's speed dropped. They strained their ears to catch sounds telling them they had come to a fishing village, but all they could hear was the engine, the water and seagulls.

'Gull Island,' Megan thought. 'Greg was right the first time.'

The engine slowed to a rhythmic throbbing and the boat rode the waves. The children huddled in stuffy darkness, rigidly silent. Andy gasped for air. Greg's knees were digging into Megan's ribs.

The engine stopped. Waves rocked the boat. They waited. Andy raised the edge of the sheeting with a finger, to breathe. Greg tried to wiggle his numbed feet. Megan's heart thumped.

Then all too soon, despite their discomfort, they heard footsteps in the stern of the Hot Stuff. They clenched their fists and held their breath. The footsteps stopped. Megan thought her heart stopped as she strained to pick up sounds; a light scraping as Alan Wetherton picked up the fishing rod, the reel spinning, a tackle box opening, an annoyed exclamation when something tinkled on the boards, and a brief scrabbling sound as it was retrieved. A grunt and a swish followed by a faint 'splish' as the line entered the water, and silence.

'He's fishing,' thought Megan. 'All this is for nothing. He's just fishing.' And they dared not move. An hour passed. Waves rippled past. Alan Wetherton sighed. No catch so far.

The line was reeled in. The tackle box opened and closed and the rod was dropped on the boards.

'He's given up,' thought Megan. 'We can go home!'

She heard footsteps going back to the cabin; the engine spluttered and revved and the skiff jerked forward.

'Thank God for that,' said Andy, raising the waterproofing and gulping air, while Greg shifted his legs and began to massage them.

'Careful,' warned Megan. 'He may look round.'

But the engine continued unchecked, the boat cut through the water and Greg groaned as his leg throbbed and tingled.

'We must be going back,' said Andy. 'So all he was doing was fishing after all.'

'Well he's finishing earlier tonight than he did last night,' said Megan, just as the engine died.

Again they froze in silence, listening, but could only hear waves against the boat.

'Just another fishing spot,' whispered Andy, but it occurred to Megan that the boat had not turned.

'We're just further on,' she thought, and held her breath as the footsteps approached again.

Alan Wetherton strode to the stern of the 'Hot Stuff,' muttering and grunting as he pulled something. The rowing boat jerked and bumped against the stern of the launch and rocked as he stepped aboard and lodged the oars into the row-locks. Only centimetres away he settled himself on the central seat, skulled to turn the boat and, pulling on the oars, moved off, taking the petrified children with him.

## Chapter Fifteen
## The Saving Bell
## AD 994

The feast was at its height. A long line of dancers was weaving in and out of the watchers, as they clapped and stamped to the rhythm of the drums. Embers glowed under the spit roasts, and the heavy fragrance of mead laced the soft air.

Gylan and Margiad stumbled into the group of musicians shouting as they came. 'The raiders are coming! Stop! Stop! The raiders are here!'

But the piper grinned at them and the others played on, their feet pounding the beat, their eyes watching each other in absorbed concentration.

Gylan turned, searching the crowds for his parents, but the chain of dancers wound round in a long snake and he couldn't see them.

Margiad grabbed his arm and pointed. 'Gyffes is yonder with Cadoc,' she shouted. 'I'll go and find Eywy or Mahme,' and she was gone, searching among the dancers, till the whirling throng closed around her.

Gylan's voice was hoarse, and his throat dry from fear and running. He pushed through the merrymakers, sobbing with exhaustion and frustration until he found his father, and hauled at the crimson cloak. Gyffes swung round.

'Gylan! Did he like the mead?'

Words would not come. Gylan held out Morwenna's brooch and Gyffes grasped his wrist and stared.

'They're coming?'

'On the horizon…Idwal'll ring the bell…at the last moment… make them come to the monastery …first.'

Gyffes turned. He lifted his head and roared like a lion.

'Stop your feasting now!'

The music faltered and continued. Gyffes filled his lungs and blasted, '*Stop I say! Stop and listen to me!*'

Startled, ragged quiet. 'The raiders are coming. You know what to do.'

The nightmare was real. Somebody screamed. Frightened gibberings rose like a tide.

'You know what to do!' Gyffes thundered again. 'Do it now!'

The snake disintegrated. Mothers called their children and hurried to fetch the livestock, while men ran for their weapons.

Gyffes grasped the shoulders of his twelve year old son. 'Go with your mother and sister,' he ordered. But Gylan looked back at him. 'I'm going to fill the cauldrons,' he said. 'It'll make someone free to fight.'

Gyffes hesitated, then clapped Gylan on the back and said, 'Go then. Take care son.'

'And you!' cried Gylan to the departing giant and forced his tired legs to run to the fortifications.

Already Mervyn was shovelling the spit roast embers on to the kindling under the cauldrons. Someone up on the fortifications ran along the high walkway, releasing the pulley chains with their big hooks that would haul them up when the water or fat boiled. Gylan stuck Morwenna's brooch inside his tunic, and helped Mervyn lift a cauldron filled with stinking animal fat over the next fire heap, backing away as the fire stoker scooped glowing embers onto the kindling underneath. Then he grasped two leather buckets and made for the river.

# The Saving Bell

Branoc and Conan were running to the bridge, and then he saw Margiad, pulling her little brother with one hand and two goats with the other, and cried out, 'God be with you!'

'Gylan come with us!' she gasped, halting and causing Eben and the goats to collide.

'I'm filling the buckets!'

He could see horror on her face, but resolution too.

'Then God be with you! We'll see you soon,' she said, tears filling her eyes as she turned and ran on.

Gylan stared after her, clinging to the last glimpse of her bright hair as she dragged her charges across the bridge in the direction of the forest, and then he lowered the buckets into the dark water.

# Idwal's Bell

Men were running to the ladders, carrying bows and arrows, swords and spears. Gylan struggled to the far cauldron with his load and at that moment, the monastery bell rang out, distant yet clear on the westerly breeze.

'God keep you Idwal,' he prayed and grabbed two more buckets. All along the fortifications encircling the little village, men took their positions, propping their weapons at their sides between stacks of heavy stones. Soon Gyffes called for silence. And in silence they waited, fear, adrenalin and discipline turning their tired arms and legs into muscled limbs of ready energy, hearts thudding, throats taut, eyes fixed on the bare cliff path.

As the bell rang out boldly, distracting the oncoming Vikings from the river mouth, Gylan hurried back and forth between the river and the cauldrons, vivid pictures jumping in his imagination. Almost he could see the dreaded raiders, faltering and wondering, their anger rising at the tell-tale warning echoing frenziedly and unstoppably from the top of the tower; see the proud dragon ships cutting through the water, their oars dipping faster and bow waves rippling deeper as they gathered speed, skimming into Monastery Cove with twelve lines of emblazoned shields flaming in the blood red sun.

# The Saving Bell

He put two buckets by a bubbling cauldron and panted for breath. His fists cleared welling tears and smoke from his eyes and, taking two more buckets he turned again from the heat of the fire towards the river, but a hand grasped his shoulder.

'Get more wood!' shouted the fire stoker. 'We'll scald the pants off 'em yet! And shut the far gates. You'll have to climb up and lower the buckets on ropes from now on!'

As he returned loaded with logs, the bell ceased, its dying echoes drowned by the yelling and crackling that filled the air over the cliffs. He climbed the fortifications and watched in horror as a pall of purple smoke plumed into the sky above the path. An ominous glow flickered, flared and spread, dancing evilly on the shields and helmets of the Vikings, as they topped the rise, and, howling like angry demons and brandishing swords and axes charged vengefully down on the waiting village.

## Chapter Sixteen
## Gull Island

The oars creaked in the rowlocks for what seemed like hours, but in fact it was only a few minutes. Megan curled trembling with the outboard digging into her back, terrified Alan Wetherton would decide to use it, but quiet was more important than speed. Would he realise the boat was heavier than usual? He was preoccupied with his destination, for soon they glided ashore, where he shipped the oars, vaulted out and tugged the boat once to beach it.

The children huddled small, listening to the retreating footsteps, and then Andy raised the edge of the sheeting and Megan wriggled round to peer out. Directly in front of them a rugged mass rose into the indigo sky. Behind them glimmered the inky sea and the gently rocking shape of the motor launch and to their left, Alan Wetherton strode along the beach towards a rocky outcrop.

'We're on the seaward side of the island,' she whispered, ducking under the sheeting. 'He's heading towards some rocks. We can get out.'

Andy pushed back the plastic sheet and they all breathed in the clean air. Faint stars pricked the sky and the retreating tide lapped against the stern of the boat.

'What shall we do?' whispered Megan.

'Can you drive the motor boat Greg?' asked Andy.

'No,' said Greg. 'It'll handle differently from my Dad's boat.'

'Okay. We'll have to take the rowing boat back.'

'And leave him stranded on the island?' breathed Megan.

'He won't be,' said Greg. 'He can swim out to the Hot Stuff from here.'

'We can't go into St Idwal's,' said Greg. 'The tide's running out by now and the current from the river's dangerous.'

'Can't we do it using the outboard?'

'No,' said Greg again. 'I don't know the waters well enough and it's dark. We'll have to go into Monastery Cove.'

'But that's probably where he's going,' pointed out Megan.

'I know,' said Greg, 'but he'll have to swim to the launch first.'

'Listen!' hissed Megan

'But if we row back into St. Idwal's we would at least have a head start,' said Andy.

From beyond the rocks came the throbbing of another boat engine.

'Now what?' wondered Andy.

'Let's go and see,' said Greg. 'Come on! We can follow Witherguts and see what's going on.'

'Keep well back,' Megan warned.

'Sure, but he doesn't know we're here.'

They climbed out the boat one after the other. Already she rested beyond the water's edge. Megan glanced at the crest of the island and noticed the sky was paler there. The beach was in deep shadow.

'C'mon,' said Greg and they crept over the thin shingle, sinking it into the wet sand. The sound of the boat engine was coming closer, and they saw a figure silhouetted on the skyline at the top of the rocks. Moments later it disappeared.

'He's gone down the other side,' whispered Andy, and broke into a cautious run, but further on the stones were bigger, and they picked their way in the blackness.

# Gull Island

Greg reached the pile of rocks first. It was about ten metres high and stretched from the main part of the island into the sea, but it was not sheer and he discovered a narrow path Alan Wetherton must have used, twining its way up through the larger boulders. Stopping every few seconds to listen, they groped their way to the top, where they crouched to look down the other side.

Only five metres below them, the man stooped among the rocks, looking out to sea. Megan had just made out the dark shape of another launch approaching when its engine died. Alan Wetherton's phone flared into life and they could see his profile lit by the screen. He leaned forward and spoke, then pocketed the phone.

He stood up and the three children huddled closer to the rocks, as they watched him tread down towards the tiny inlet below. He crossed the tongue of sand and to wait by the water's edge, in the light reflected from the sea.

'What are they doing?' asked Megan, puzzled.

'Bringing in the drink cartons,' said Andy, 'except they're not really drink cartons.'

''Course not,' muttered Greg. 'He's smuggling drugs! Dad said the police searched all the fishing boats in Tremarron a few weeks ago 'cos they think drugs are coming in along this coast.'

'I know!' said Andy. 'The helper stuffs the drugs in a secret pocket in the trekkers' saddle bags, and they carry them back to Wetherton's place.'

'But they don't know!' chimed in Greg. 'And when he hides the next lot in the old kitchen, he burns the empty cartons in the fireplace!'

'No wonder he doesn't want the monastery to become a museum,' said Megan.

'Sh!' Said Greg. 'There's a rowing boat coming in.'

They watched in silence as the oarsman jumped out and pulled the boat ashore. The stranger leaned into the boat and lifted out a deep rectangular shape and handed it to Alan Wetherton who turned and carried it towards the rocks, disappearing from view.

'There you go!' exclaimed Andy.

'We can't stay here!' hissed Megan. 'We've got to go now!'

'Hang on,' muttered Greg, his eyes fixed on the men. 'He's going back for more. They must store them here somewhere, and Witherguts brings them over a couple of trays at a time. There aren't enough ponies to take that lot all at once!'

'May be there's a cave,' suggested Andy.

'Must be,' said Greg.

Alan Wetherton made three journeys to and from the rowing boat and then, taking one last tray he lifted a hand briefly to the other man.

'Come on!' said Megan. 'Quick!'
Already he was walking up the sand to the tumble of rocks, with the last load in his hands.

Megan, Andy and Greg wriggled round to scramble back down the rugged path. Tiny pieces of shale scraped free and rolled and scuttered to the beach below.

'Careful!' warned Greg, as they felt their way down.

'He'll see us,' gasped Megan in rising panic and she slipped and slithered, sending more loose stones rattling and bouncing down to the sand.

'Idiot!' warned Andy.

Almost falling over one another they crunched down onto the shingle and stumbled seawards by the edge of the rocks before splashing along the sodden shoreline towards the boat. They had almost reached her when the moon rose over the crest of the island and flooded the beach with its pale light.

'Stinking sturgeon!' gasped Greg. 'Run for it!'

## Idwal's Bell

Their footprints left pools of darkness in the wet sand. They grasped the bows and shoved the boat towards the shallow waves when, 'Bloody kids! Get off that boat!' roared from behind them.

'Push!' yelled Andy, but the receding tide had left the boat dry on the sand.

There was another shout and Megan glanced up. Alan Wetherton waved his arms and disappeared.

'He's calling the other guy,' she wailed. 'They'll chase us! Heave!'

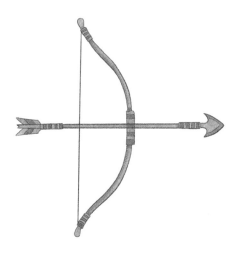

## Chapter Seventeen
## St. Idwals

The Vikings, bent on plunder and revenge attacked with ferocious efficiency, hastened by failing light, and outraged to find the village fortified and prepared. They lit fires and shot flaming arrows over the palisade while some of them hacked at the wooden piers, doggedly withstanding the cascade of arrows and stones hailing down on them. Many climbed the defences and Gylan, glimpsing a helmet silhouetted high above him, thought all was lost, when the first cauldron of boiling fat poured down and he felt the hair on his scalp rise as screams of pain tore the air above the noise of battle.

## Idwal's Bell

Shaking, he climbed a ladder on the other side of the village to lean over the palisade and lower his buckets into the river, only to be punched into its inky depths by a body plummeting down from behind him. He floundered under its weight, swallowing water, gasping at the cold and trapped by heavy arms and legs. Pushing upwards he saw the fortifications looming above him as the river swept him onwards. He wrapped his arms round a bridge pile and clung on, watching with horror stretched eyes as Brythen's body struck against struts and piers before swirling with one of the buckets into the furore of the current.

Gylan retched as blood and water pulled and sucked past him and fighting on the edge of certain death, he clawed his way from pile to pile while the river tried to tear his numb fingers from their grasp and squeezed his lungs with its eddying force. He sucked air, coughed out muddy water and stared frantically upwards through blurring vision and for a moment saw Margiad, red curls about her white face, leaning over and shouting to him. Chest heaving, he struck out for the bank, dug his fingers into slippery mud and hung on while the battle roared and clashed on the other side of the village, until he gathered the strength to haul himself out of the river and stagger back to his remaining bucket with water running from every part of him.

More screams as more cauldrons were tipped. Bodies fell from either side, some into the water but others with a sickening crunch on to the land.

Gylan pulled the bucket on its rope from the water, but a hand reached up and grasped it. He screamed and clenched a fist to beat it off when Cadoc's head surfaced, coughing and gulping air, and with huge relief washing over him, Gylan hauled him ashore.

'Are you hurt?' he yelled, but Cadoc shook his head. 'Went in further up, but they'll soon be round this side,' and gasping in breath he shouted up the fortifications for the rope to be secured. A hand waved in acknowledgement and Cadoc lifted Gylan.

'Go on,' he said, and Gylan wrapped his feet round the rope and pulled and pushed his way to the top with a strength he didn't know he possessed. As soon as he tumbled over the palisade onto the walkway, Cadoc followed him and without another word strode back to retrieve his bow, while Gylan swung the bucket into the river. He pulled it up, climbed down to the nearest cauldron and slopped in the water.

And so he struggled for what seemed eternity. For the nightmare his mother had tried to keep from him was here and alive. The horror carved forever in the memories of Idwal and Gyffes had returned, and they must all fight or die.

Back and forth he hurried, sometimes to fetch wood and others to fetch water. He hauled on the winch wheels to help send the cauldrons of bubbling fat or water upwards, steeling himself against the shrieks of agony as the boiling liquid poured over the Vikings climbing the barriers. Sick with the stench of blood and mud and scalded with steam he saw his hands bled from pulling the ropes and the winch, and with weird elation knew it didn't hurt, that he was living on a high plain of energy, intoxicated with utmost fear and driven determination.

For those three dreadful hours the clashing of metal and the cries of battle battered his ears. Gylan supported injured men to shelter where some of the older men bound their wounds. Ghastly screams and heavy splashes resounded as men fell from the fortifications into the river. Some of them struggled ashore; others disappeared into the strong current and were carried out to sea. From the Monastery side came relentless chopping sounds as a group of Vikings strove to axe the juddering wooden piers. A burning arrow crunched into the thatch of a hut in the centre of the village and flames flared and spread. Panic welled up inside Gylan but he quelled it, sobbing with exhaustion and distress. Still he toiled, terrified the raiders would ransack the village and slaughter them all. A spear thudded into the earth next to him. He yanked it out and wedged it into the chain on a cauldron.

Then a stunning blow on his back sent him sprawling face down with the fire stoker next to him. He struggled up, clawing mud from his eyes, and saw a second spear quivering in the earth where he had been standing. The fire stoker got up and extended a filthy hand.

'Up now,' he shouted above the clamour. 'Watch out for the next one.' And he turned to push more wood under a cauldron. Everything was blurred. Gylan's legs were lead. He heaved on the pulley wheel with Mervyn, his bleeding hands gripping with their last strength. From the other side of the fortifications a horn sounded. The Vikings roared and some of the roaring changed to shrieks as boiling water scalded them. Gylan crumpled where he stood, his lungs straining for air. The horn wailed again and his father's voice thundered above the din.

'Porthros! Hold your ground! Hold fast!'

Gylan looked up, eyes streaming with the smoke from the fires. Against the dark sky the men of Porthros released their bowstrings and a shower of arrows sung down upon the Vikings. Hoarse voices howled in pain and dismay.

'Again!'

More arrows, more boiling water. Gylan struggled to his feet and leant his weight on a chain. Shouts of excitement. Everything spinning. Mervyn grabbed him and pushed him away from the fires.

'Sit down lad. The battle is ours!'

'What?' He scrambled up again and strained to listen to the leaders commanding the Porthros men to stay on the fortifications. Unbelievably the sounds of battle were lessening. He waited, his chest heaving for breath.

Bowstrings stretched and arrows rained downwards. Voices in a strange language bellowed commands. The pandemonium diminished. Wounded men groaned and weary footsteps stumbled. Someone waded unsteadily into the river and hauled something out. Gylan's legs buckled beneath him.

A resounding cheer went up from the fortifications and swelled like a storm as the defeated raiders gathered their stricken men and staggered in a broken line up the path to the cliffs.

Gylan sat with his head bowed on his knees while the men of Porthros clapped each other on the back and cheered their triumph.

'Gylan!' cried Gyffes, picking him up and burying his head in the boy's chest. 'Oh what a son I have!'

Gylan slid his arms around him and felt the blood on his shoulder.

'You're injured!'

'Only a few scrapes and bruises. 'Tis Cadoc's blood.'

'Is he…?'

'Wounded. He'll survive.'

'Poor Brythen….'

'I know.'

'And Father…Idwal.'

'We'll go now. That horde will put to sea, what's left of them.' He turned. 'Come Mervyn and Petroc.' The monk hurried towards him, carrying a burning torch. 'We're going to find Idwal. Come with us,' and Gyffes grasped another flaming torch from the foot of the fortifications and handed it to Gylan.

He pushed his son up the wooden ladder before him and the monk, the fire stoker and Mervyn followed them.

'Where to Gyffes?' asked someone on the fortifications.

'To find Idwal,' said Gyffes, and more men joined them, climbing down the ladders, picking their way through mud, bodies and broken weapons at the bottom, and hurrying in weary and anxious procession up the path to the monastery, the torchlight ruddying their tousled hair and tattered clothing.

They passed the remains of the empty homes, blackened and still smoking. The monastery was silent, the bell tower dark against the starry sky and from somewhere Gylan's legs found strength enough to run ahead.

## Idwal's Bell

'Gylan!' shouted Gyffes, but Gylan, torch held high, ignored him, plunging recklessly into the cell by the tower.

'Idwal! Idwal!'

He lay face downwards, the bell rope, hacked down by his enemy, still grasped in his hands. A scarlet stain had soaked his rough, woollen habit and pooled on the stone floor.

'Idwal!' cried Gylan, tears pouring down his haggard, soot grimed cheeks. Gyffes tried to pull him back, but Gylan wrenched himself free, dropped his torch, and was on his knees beside his uncle and friend, trying to chafe life back into the cold hands. Others crowded into the little cell. Petroc and two other monks knelt beside Idwal, and Mervyn silently took the torches while Gyffes pulled Gylan to his feet.

But Gylan rounded on all of them, his face distorted with anger and grief.

'He saved us! And now he's dead!' He clenched his fists. 'You all laughed at him but he's died for us. You said they'd never come again. You moaned when he made us build things.' He gasped, wiping his arm across his eyes. 'But it's saved us. He wouldn't come with Margiad and me. He stayed to ring the bell. He did that for us, and they've killed him.' He shook his fists. 'They've killed him!' And he sank to his knees next to Idwal's inert body and sobbed.

There was silence. Those outside the little cell heard Gylan's rage, and stood with heads bowed, the torchlight flickering in the spring night, while triumph splintered into tragedy.

'He saved us,' sobbed Gylan again. 'He saved all of us here, and all the ones up in the forest. And the animals. People laughed at him, but he saved us.'

'He surely did,' agreed Mervyn, 'for all our moans and grumbles.'

'Cadoc and me more than once,' said Morgan. 'He was a brave man.'

'He said the village was worth fighting for,' cried Gylan, lifting his head. 'He wanted to keep us safe.'

'And he did,' said Gyffes. 'It's what he believed in.' He knelt and held his son close. 'And so everyone knows what he did, we'll rename the village after him. God grant him peace now with Morwenna.' His voice broke and he pressed his cheek on Gylan's scorched and tangled hair. Petroc crossed himself and laid his crucifix on Idwal's bloodied back.

'We'll write down his story,' he promised, 'and it'll be preserved forever, so that men will honour his courage and his sacrifice.'

He bowed his head.

## Idwal's Bell

Five days later, Gylan and Margiad sat on the riverbank. Men were working on the battered fortifications, replacing damaged struts with strong seasoned wood stored for the purpose. Children walked along the river's edge, searching for momentos.

'Sometimes I can't believe it,' said Margiad. 'All my life I've dreaded it and now it's happened. And I'm still here thanks to Idwal and all the people who fought. Thank you Gylan, for all you did. You did know what to do.'

'We wouldn't have done any of it if Idwal hadn't made us prepare,' said Gylan. 'The monastery wouldn't have been there, nor the bell tower or the empty homes that slowed them down.'

'I can't believe he's gone,' said Margiad, blinking away tears. 'I keep expecting to see him walking down to talk to your father…'

'…or sitting up by the waterfall,' said Gylan in a husky voice. 'I always knew where to find him.' Margiad was silent for a moment, but then she said, 'He loved you.'

'And I loved him,' said Gylan, 'but he loved all of us. He loved the village. He said it was a good place to be.'

He reached inside his tunic, brought out the woven silver brooch and held it in the flat of his hand in his lap. Margiad leaned forward and touched it gently.

'His wedding gift to Morwenna.'

Gylan nodded.

'It's beautiful. You must keep it.'

'Petroc copied the design to decorate the story and he and my father said I should keep it, but I'm not sure.'

'Why not? Idwal would be pleased for you to have it.'

'I'd like to keep it, but I have this feeling...' His voice trailed away and he gazed out past the river mouth and the headland to the open sea, remembering that golden evening when tiny specks had broken the line of the horizon. He shuddered, seeing Idwal at the head of the waterfall, an undaunted figure watching alone as the Vikings approached.

A tear splashed on the silver brooch.

'He said he would always be with us. That some part of him would always be watching.'

He stood up.

## Idwal's Bell

'I know what to do,' he said, holding out his hand. 'Come with me Margiad.'

She scrambled to her feet, and with Morwenna's brooch once more clutched firmly in Gylan's right hand, they set off together up the path to the top of the cliff.

## Chapter Eighteen
## Something Sharp

With cold sea swirling about their legs, Andy, Megan and Greg pushed the rowing boat deeper into the water and flung themselves aboard, tipping her dangerously. Megan fumbled for an oar while Andy wobbled astern to the outboard. Driving his oar into the sand, Greg pushed off and then scrambled to a seat, shouting, 'Keep your back to the bows! Okay! Together!'

Valiantly Megan tried to copy him, leaning forward and heaving back on the oar and they manoeuvred inexpertly southwards to skirt the island while Andy pulled time and again on the motor cord. Nothing happened. The men's outboard roared and echoed against the rocks.

'Rats! Get on with it, Andy!' begged Greg hauling on his oar.

'Won't start!' gasped Andy, yanking the cord again.

'Have you switched on the petrol?'

'What?'

'Switch on the petrol!'

'Where?'

'Knob with a bar across it down on one side.'

The other outboard grew louder. Andy's groping fingers found a round knob. He twisted the bar and pulled the cord again. The engine coughed.

'Come on Andy!'

Again, he pulled. The men's boat swung round the rocky outcrop.

'You do it!'

Andy grabbed the oar and Greg ducked to the stern, working at the engine as Andy and Megan pulled the oars. They were moving faster now, but Greg yanked the cord and at last the outboard buzzed into action.

'Ship the oars!' he commanded, and the boat plunged forwards. Megan clutched the side as she slipped sternwards and swivelled her oar up into the boat.

# Something Sharp

'Hang on!' Greg accelerated and Megan gasped as the bows slapped against a wave, showering them with spray, just as Andy saw the other boat leaping through the water towards them.

'Go on Greg!' he urged. 'They're gaining!'

'Stinking sturgeon,' muttered Greg and accelerated again, concentrating grimly as they negotiated the island's rocky shore, heading eastwards towards Monastery Cove. The bows smacked against the receding tide and the wind lifted their hair. Megan gripped the rowlock with one hand and Andy hung on to the other. Megan's teeth clenched as she turned round, searching the dark for Monastery Cove. The moon blanched the monastery arches and highlighted the bell tower like a finger against the sky. She looked back to the pursuing boat racing through the water behind them, its silver bow wave rippling deeper as it gathered speed.

*They're gaining*, she thought. *They'll catch us!*

She turned huge eyes towards Andy and yelled above the engine, 'There are three of us and only two of them. They can't catch us all.'

Andy stared at her and then shouted to Greg. 'Take us in to the shallows and go out again. I'll bol for the path and get help. Megan run left along the shore and hide.'

Greg looked hard at Andy, thinking, and nodded. Megan shook her brother's arm. 'Take care,' she pleaded.

'You too,' he shouted back. 'Hide and sit tight. I can beat them up the cliff path.'

Greg's jaw set with concentration as he stared ahead. 'You'll have to jump,' he warned, and they nodded, watching the skimming boat behind. The beach rolled out and the cliffs rose before them. At the last moment Greg hauled on the tiller as far as he dared, and the boat swerved to port, leaving a widening field of silver foam as one each side, Megan and Andy plunged into the water.

Gasping with cold they heard Greg accelerate away and the other boat snarl towards them and then swing after him, the men cursing in frustration and anger. There was a splash as Alan Wetherton leapt into the sea and as the boats swept away came the desperate race to the shore. Staggering through shallow waves, Andy drove his legs to run for the cliff path while Megan veered left, fleeing along the moonlit beach. Alan Wetherton hesitated and then tore after Andy to head him off before he could fetch help. Megan glanced upwards and glimpsed a tall figure standing against the starred sky above the waterfall.

'Tom!' she yelled. 'Tom! Help us!'

## Something Sharp

For a strange moment she thought he hadn't heard, but then he ran across the top of the cliff towards the bell tower, and she realised in mounting horror that Alan Wetherton had turned to chase her. Panic sent her across the beach like a deer. She splashed through the stream and headed towards the cliffs to hide amongst the rocks in their shadow, but he was on her heels.

Greg's voice rang in her ears: 'Some bits are not so steep; then it's easy…' and she pounded towards the cliff, stumbling on the stones before grasping unseen handholds and hauling herself up with the waterfall thundering to her right. She searched for niches and crannies as she struggled upwards, praying Tom would return. She could hear her pursuer scrabbling behind, drove herself faster, and slipped, her stomach clenching as she swung perilously outwards, her feet paddling empty air, but she grasped a tamarisk branch and clutched at the cliff face.

# Idwal's Bell

She was halfway up when the bell rang out, chiming loudly and repeatedly, echoing over the rocks, the shore and the sea. Her lungs were sore, her fingers bled and she was half blinded by cold spray. Ducking her head as she climbed, she saw the man's upturned face twisted with fury only centimetres below her, and with fear choking her throat she tightened her hand hold and clung on as he grabbed her right foot. She kicked out, her fingers sliding on the slippery rocks as he gained on her, seizing her leg and dragging her downwards. She reached out wildly with her right hand, whimpering with frustration as it plunged into a space behind the waterfall.

Water spurted over her arm and back, but she found loose shale, grasped it and hurled it over the man's face as he hauled at her. Hanging on with her left fingertips she plunged her right hand in further, found a larger stone and threw that. This time he shouted, and his hold slipped but he didn't let go. Panic stormed inside her and she reached in again, grasping something hard and sharp. He was gripping her leg, clawing her skin.

Her left hand was slipping, as sobbing with fright she swung her right hand down with all her strength and stabbed his arm.

# Something Sharp

He howled in pain, and his grip slackened. She kicked and he let go and slithered downwards, bumping and sliding to the bottom. Unable to move she bowed her head and clung to the cliff like a spider halfway up a bath, her stomach churning and her limbs trembling as spray showered over her.

In the bay, the two outboards were moaning in incessant circles, the one in pursuit of the other. Everything was spinning. The bell ceased. Shadows crept across her vision and she tried to blink them away. In the distance was a wailing sound. She hung on, only half conscious. A light flickered across the sky. Voices. Summoning all her strength she filled her lungs and shouted '*Help me somebody! Please help me!*

Nobody. Easier to let go. She slipped, but the sharp thing jabbed the palm of her hand and jerked her awake.

'*Help me, please help me!*' She gasped for air and shouted again. '*Here! By the waterfall!*' Tom should have guessed. He should have realised. '*Tom! Tom! I'm here! Help me!*' And a silhouette appeared above her, blotting out the moon.

'Okay. Hang on there. We're here.'

'Help Greg,' she gasped. 'In the boat.'

'Don't worry. He'll be okay. Let's get you up.'

She waited numbly, not realising there were two people, only that both her wrists were grasped, her shoulders supported and she was gently raised to the top of the cliff. A jumper was flung over her head. A police car wailed to a halt beside the bell tower. There were shouted instructions and seconds later the sound of footsteps running down the cliff path to the beach. More shouts and one outboard motor became fainter and fainter while one slowed and chugged closer.

'Megs! Megs! Where are you?'

She rolled over and sat up to see Andy running across the cliff top.

'Megs! You okay?'

'Yes,' she croaked, and turned to her rescuers. 'Thank you,' she said, not recognising either of them. 'Thank you very much.'

## Chapter Nineteen
## Idwal All The Time

Half an hour later, Auntie Liz's kitchen was full of people. Megan, Andy and Greg sat at the table, swathed in dressing gowns, while Mum, Greg's mother and his father, still in his work clothes and smelling of fish, a policeman, a woman police constable and the two house guests all sat at the table or on kitchen stools, trying to piece together what had happened. As the kettle boiled, Tom Merthen produced mugs of tea and handed them round.

Tired and confused the children told their story, from their first suspicions, through their investigations, to their frightening adventure that night, while the policeman tapped at a laptop.

'You'll have to go through this again,' he said. 'I haven't got it straight.'

'What about the other man?' asked Greg. 'The one that got away?'

'We'll get him,' came the reply. 'We've put out a call for private boat movements to be watched. He'll turn up sometime, even if it's in France. Now you say,' he turned to Andy, 'that you jumped out the boat and headed towards the cliff path to raise the alarm.'

Andy nodded.

'And Alan Wetherton came after you?'

'Yes. We knew they couldn't follow all of us, so we split up. Megs went left to hide in the rocks.'

The policeman turned to Megan. 'And what made him come after you instead?'

'I saw Tom at the top of the waterfall and shouted at him to come and help. Then I saw him run across to the bell tower.' She saw Tom shake his head, but she carried on. 'He was trying to stop me getting to Tom. Greg said he climbs the cliffs sometimes, so I decided to climb them to get to Tom.'

'Wow!' muttered Andy. 'Awesome.'

Greg did a thumbs up to Megan.

'And he followed?' said the policeman, concentrating on his typing.

'Yes. I started to climb next to the waterfall. I heard the bell ringing when I was about halfway up…' Tom shook his head again, 'and I thought Tom would come back, but Alan Wetherton followed me up the cliff.' She stopped, remembering the fear welling inside her as she struggled upwards.

'And?' said the policeman, while Mum quietly handed her a mug of tea and put an arm round her.

She took the tea in her left hand and sipped gratefully.

'He climbed faster than I did,' she said, and told how he had grabbed her and how she had tried to shake him off. Everyone murmured as she stopped and drank again.

'I tried to grab a rock with my right hand to pull myself higher, but my hand went into a hole behind the water, so I got hold of some loose stones from there and threw them at him, twice. He still had hold of my leg so I tried again and there was something sharp in the hole so I pulled it out and leant down and stabbed him. That's when he let go and slipped down the cliff. Then I shouted again and these people found me.'

She smiled at the two guests sitting wide eyed on the other side of the table.

'You said 'something sharp,'' said the policeman, still tapping. 'What was it? Do you know?'

Megan opened her right hand. 'This,' she said.

With one movement Tom Merthen was kneeling beside her, gently holding her wrist and staring open mouthed at the round tarnished latticed brooch lying daubed with mud and bloodstains in the centre of her palm. He wiped the mud away to reveal the smooth gemstones set in the blackened, woven silver and the long sharp pin. For a few seconds he was bereft of speech, then he looked up at her.

'You found this,' he croaked, 'behind the waterfall?'

Megan nodded.

'Do you know what it is, Sir?' asked the policeman painstakingly. 'Can you tell us?'

Tom shook his head again, hardly able to speak. 'I'm not sure. Yet it must be - it's incredible – I can't believe…' He stopped and then tried again. 'We have part of an illuminated manuscript telling Idwal's story. It's been preserved, what's left of it. I told you…' He looked at the three children and they nodded. 'We know Idwal kept a brooch belonging to his wife after she was killed by the Vikings. This design,' he pointed to the brooch, 'is on the manuscript several times. We wondered if it was the brooch, but now there's no doubt. It must have been put behind the waterfall after Idwal's death.'

'To keep watch,' said Andy.

'Maybe,' said Tom. 'Yes. To keep watch. How extraordinary that Megan should find it now!'

'There's one thing,' said the policeman, still typing. 'I understand Mrs Williams had only just come home, and you sir,' he said to Tom, 'were on your way with Greg's parents to tell Andy and Megan's mother that you'd found Greg's bag by the lifeboat steps, when this young man,' he nodded, indicating Andy,' came running down to fetch help. Yet Megan says she saw you at the top of the water-fall and called to you for help.'

Tom shook his head yet again. 'I was going to say,' he said, 'that's most peculiar. I wasn't at the top of the cliffs. I didn't ring the bell because…'

'I thought Andy rang the bell,' chimed in Greg.

## Idwal's Bell

'I didn't,' said Andy. 'It was already ringing when I ran past, and Mum and the guests had heard it and were on their way before I reached the house.'

'He couldn't have rung it,' put in Tom.

'Then how…?'

'Someone must have,' said Mum.

'But they couldn't,' insisted Tom. 'There is no bell!'

'What?' gasped everyone together.

'There is no bell,' repeated Tom. 'The bell tower is locked because the stairs are unsafe. There hasn't been a bell for centuries.'

There was a dumbfounded silence.

'But,' said Andy after a few moments, 'Megan says she's heard it before.'

Everyone turned to look at Megan, who sat staring at the precious silver brooch in her hand.

'I did,' she said. 'Twice. And I know who was ringing it. It was Idwal. It was Idwal I saw on the cliff top. It was Idwal all the time.'

## Chapter Twenty
## At The Waterfall

'So the fortune teller was not so daft after all,' said Greg the next day, as he, Andy and Megan tramped up the track to the top of the cliffs after tea. They had slept most of the day but had been revived by food and had come to look again at the scene of all the excitement.

'Maybe be not,' said Andy. 'I still don't believe it was anything more than luck.'

'But there was even something round and sharp,' said Greg. 'The brooch.'

'Sure. But it could have been a stone.'

'But even you said the brooch must have been put at the top of the waterfall to keep watch,' pointed out Megan.

'That's different,' said Andy, and Megan and Greg hooted with laughter.

## Idwal's Bell

'Do you believe me now when I say I heard the bell ring twice before?' demanded Megan.

'Since we all heard it the third time, I have to,' admitted Andy. 'Something made you get me out of bed the other night.'

'And what about my seeing Tom at the top of the waterfall last night when he wasn't there?'

'Well, I've never believed in ghosts, but I know some people swear they've seen them,' said Andy.

'You're avoiding answering the question,' said Greg. 'You'll probably grow up to be a politician!'

'I'm not denying we all heard a bell last night,' said Andy. 'I've agreed everybody heard it.'

'A bell that isn't there,' said Greg with relish. 'Amazing!' He turned and waved as they passed the bell tower. 'Hey Bell Tower! D'you hear? You're amazing!'

'Maybe people's will stays in a place,' conceded Andy. 'If you want something badly enough, maybe the want stays for a long time. Idwal desperately wanted to protect the village, so maybe his will is still protecting it.'

'Whatever it is,' stated Greg, 'it's amazing that Megan found the brooch last night, just when she needed it most. I bet it gave Witherguts a nasty shock when you turned round and stabbed his arm!'

'He was probably more surprised than hurt,' said Megan, 'but he must have lots of bruises after sliding down the cliff.'

'To be collected by a couple of policemen,' giggled Greg.

'And now the monastery can be used for the good of the village again,' said Andy with satisfaction. 'I bet Idwal's pleased.'

They reached the top of the waterfall and sat down looking out to Gull Island. It looked quite innocent, as if it knew nothing about smuggling. Footsteps across the grass made them turn round to see Tom Merthen approaching them, grinning.

'Hullo,' he said, sitting down next to them and putting a square parcel down on the grass. 'Your Mum said you'd be up here. Good news about the twins!'

'Great,' agreed Megan 'Everything's fine and Uncle Rob's coming back this evening and we can go and see them tomorrow.'

'Two boys,' said Andy. 'We suggested calling them Idwal and Gylan.'

Tom laughed and said, 'I gather they're to be called Simon and Patrick.'

'Yes,' said Megan.

'Well, those are good, sound names. How are you heroes?'

# Idwal's Bell

'Heroes?' said Andy. 'We've been told off for getting on the boat! We came to look at where it all happened. I can't believe we were ever on Gull Island!'

They looked across the sea to where the sky was turning to gold as the sun slid down towards the horizon.

'I'll take you there again and you can look round in daylight,' said Tom. 'In fact, the police will want you to show them where you saw the other man handing over the drugs.'

'That'll be great,' said Greg. 'I'd love to do that.'

'It wasn't great last night,' said Megan.

'No,' agreed Tom. 'You three did a great job. You've done the village a good turn as well as adding to Idwal's story. We can use that when we open the visitor centre. Which brings me to what I wanted to say. I've been talking to your parents and it's decided you must be rewarded, so think of one or two ideas and I'll do what I can.'

'Brilliant,' breathed Greg at once.

'Cool!' said Andy.

'Thank you,' said Megan.

'But,' went on Tom. 'I wanted to give Megan something special for finding that wonderful brooch and handing it back for the monastery museum.'

'Well, it may have saved my life,' said Megan.

'Indeed,' said Tom, 'but it's tremendously important to our project and I wanted to say a big thank you, so this, Megan Williams, is just for you.'

He handed her the parcel. Megan took it wonderingly and stared back at him.

'Well, open it!' said Andy. 'We want to see what it is!'

Megan tugged at the sticky tape, drew off the brown paper and revealed a large rectangular cardboard packet. She opened one end and then pulled. Out slid an artist's paintbox.

'Oh!' she gasped and opened it.

'Hey! Look at that!' exclaimed Greg.

'Wow!' said Andy. 'That's better than the one at the school fete.'

'It's beautiful,' breathed Megan. 'Tom, thank you so much! I can't believe it.'

Tom smiled and said, 'I thought if you paint some pictures of the monastery I could sell them for you in the gift shop.'

'You mean she won't have to wait a hundred years before her work is recognised?' exclaimed Greg.

'I hope not,' said Tom, startled.

'It's wonderful, Tom,' said Megan, and hugged him. 'Thank you! I must go and show Mum.' She scrambled to her feet and turned to Tom again.

# Idwal's Bell

'Thanks a million! It's great! We'll see you soon, won't we?'

'I promise a trip to the island very soon,' said Tom, standing up too.

'Come on,' said Andy, getting to his feet and pulling up Greg. 'Let's go and show Mum. See you soon Tom!' And they raced across the grass.

At the top of the path Megan stopped and turned. Tom stood facing out to sea, a tall silhouette against the golden sky, looking out to the long, straight horizon. She caught her breath.

'One day I'll paint him like that,' she promised herself. 'A big picture, and it'll hang in the monastery museum. Then everyone will know how Idwal stood, waiting for the Vikings.'

Printed in Great Britain
by Amazon